A new villain lurks in the Shadows of the Empire . . .

Luke reached out for the energy of the Force, warm and bright, and wrapped himself in it like a suit of armor. Once again, the Force was there for him.

But something else was there, too, pulling at him from the shadows, just out of reach; a hard, powerful coldness that was the opposite of what his teachers had shown him. It was the part of the Force that gave Darth Vader such power.

The dark side.

No! he thought, pushing the dark side away. He took a deep breath, drew the brightness of the Force around him again, and stepped out onto the wire. Suddenly it was effortless, as though the wire had become as wide as a public sidewalk.

Halfway across he started to run. He told himself it was part of the test. He told himself that the Force was with him, that he could rise above his father's fall to the dark side, that anything was possible to one trained as a Jedi Knight.

He tried not to believe that he ran because he could feel the dark side walking the wire behind him, its evil tracking his every step. Following him . . . and gaining.

STAR WARS®

SHADOWS OF THE EMPIRE™

A JUNIOR NOVELIZATION
BY CHRISTOPHER GOLDEN

BASED ON THE NOVEL BY STEVE PERRY

A YEARLING BOOK

Published by
Bantam Doubleday Dell Books for Young Readers
a division of
Bantam Doubleday Dell Publishing Group, Inc.
1540 Broadway
New York, New York 10036

ISBN: 0-440-41303-6

Printed in the United States of America
October 1996
OPM 10 9 8 7 6 5 4 3 2 1

To my son, Nicholas, who was eighteen months old when he became entranced by the Star Wars films—what he calls the "moon tapes"—and my wife, Connie, who sat through the trilogy with him at least a hundred times

PROLOGUE

Ancient was the one word that stuck in Xizor's head when he looked at the Emperor. He was so thin and sickly, he looked about a thousand years old. He looked half dead. But that illusion was shattered the moment he moved. The Emperor was alive, and he was the most powerful man in the galaxy.

Xizor (pronounced SHEE-zor) watched as the Emperor stepped into position for a holographic communication. With such technology, it was possible to see a three-dimensional image of the person you were speaking to, and that person could see you. But while Xizor could also see the person the Emperor was contacting, that person could not see Xizor. It pleased Xizor to know that the Emperor trusted him enough to let him stay.

The communication began. A hologram sprang to life in the center of the room. It was a man, or at least appeared to be. He was dressed all in black, with a long cloak and shining helmet, and he was down on one knee to show his obedience to the Emperor. Xizor recognized him immediately. It was Darth Vader.

Xizor hated Vader.

"What is thy bidding, my master?" Vader asked.

"There is a great disturbance in the Force," the Emperor said, red eyes glowing beneath the hood of his dark robe.

"I have felt it," Vader admitted.

"We have a new enemy," the Emperor explained. "Luke Skywalker."

Xizor was surprised to hear this. He knew that, a long time ago, Vader's name had been Skywalker. Whoever this Luke Skywalker was, Xizor knew he must be extremely important to draw the Emperor's attention. He did not let his surprise show, however. His people, the Falleen, prided themselves on their control over emotions. They were a cold, lizardlike people who looked down on what they considered inferior species.

"Yes, my master," Vader responded.

"He could destroy us," the Emperor said.

Xizor was very surprised to discover that the Emperor was afraid of something.

"He's just a boy," Vader said. "Obi-Wan can no longer help him."

When he heard the name Obi-Wan, Xizor knew that his agents had failed him. Not only had they never informed him of this Luke Skywalker, but he had been under the impression that Obi-Wan Kenobi, the legendary Jedi Knight, was dead. Xizor was furious. His agents would be severely punished for their failure.

The Emperor continued. "The Force is strong with him. The son of Skywalker must not become a Jedi."

The son of Skywalker, Xizor thought. *Vader's son? Amazing!*

"If he could be turned, he would become a powerful ally," Vader said hopefully.

"Yes . . . yes. He would be a great asset," the Emperor said. "Can it be done?"

"He will join us or die, master," Vader declared, but it was clear to Xizor that Vader was not being honest. He obviously did not want to kill his own son. Xizor was the Dark Prince, Underlord of Black Sun, the largest criminal organization in the galaxy. He didn't really understand the Force, the mysterious power that the Emperor, Darth Vader, Obi-Wan Kenobi, and now apparently this Luke Skywalker could control. But he knew how to read people. Vader wanted Skywalker alive.

Which Xizor found very interesting.

The Emperor finished his communication and turned back to face him. "Now, where were we, Prince Xizor?" he asked.

Xizor smiled. He would complete his business with the Emperor, but he would not forget the name Luke Skywalker.

1

Chewbacca roared, tossing stormtroopers around as if they were dolls. But there were too many of them. He couldn't win. Han Solo, Chewie's best friend, was about to be flash-frozen in carbonite. It might kill him. But Han stepped forward, yelling at Chewie to stop, calming him down before the stormtroopers shot the big, fur-covered Wookiee.

"Chewie, there'll be another time! The princess, you have to take care of her. D'you hear me? Huh?"

Princess Leia stared at them both, unable to move, unable to believe this was happening. They had been betrayed by Han's so-called friend, Lando Calrissian, who had handed them over to Darth Vader. Now they were in a large dark room somewhere in Cloud City, waiting for their final fate.

Blinking, Chewbacca looked at Han, at the traitor Calrissian, at the technicians and guards lined up to see if Solo would survive Vader's experiment with the carbonite. Finally he looked at Princess Leia. Then he nodded, accepting what Han had asked him to do. Chewbacca allowed the guards to put cuffs on him.

Han and Leia looked at each other. She pulled him

close; they kissed . . . and then the stormtroopers pulled him away and positioned him on the platform that would lower him into the pit.

Leia couldn't keep the words in any longer. "I love you!" she shouted.

Han nodded. "I know," he said.

The platform sank, lowering him into the pit. Han and Leia stared at one another as he went down and down, and then finally a cloud of freezing mist blocked their view. Chewie roared again, but it was more like a cry of pain than of anger.

Han! Leia shouted in her mind, trying to see through the icy fog.

Oh, Han!

Leia snapped awake from the nightmare and sat up straight. Her pulse raced as she tried to push the bad dream away. But this wasn't like other nightmares. This had actually happened. Han Solo, the man she loved, was embedded in a block of carbonite. A bounty hunter had hauled him away to some far-off corner of the galaxy.

She stared out the viewport at the stars above Tatooine and fought back tears. After all, she was Leia Organa, Princess of the Royal Family of Alderaan, elected to the Imperial Senate, a worker in the Alliance to restore the Republic. Alderaan was gone, destroyed by Vader and the Death Star; the Imperial Senate was disbanded; the Alliance was outmanned and outgunned by the Empire, ten thousand to one, but she was who she was.

She would not cry. She would get even.

It was three hours past midnight, and half the people on the planet Tatooine were asleep.

Not Luke Skywalker.

Luke stood barefoot on a platform sixty meters above the sand, staring at the tightrope that stretched out before him. He was dressed in loose-fitting black clothes, the desert wind whipping them about his body. His lightsaber had been lost during battle, when Darth Vader had severed his hand at the wrist. The hand had been replaced with a synthetic one, but the lightsaber was more complicated. Luke had been building himself a new one, but it wasn't quite ready yet.

He'd watched the high-wire acrobats performing earlier, but the carnival was done for the night. The lights under the tent were dim, and Luke was alone in the silent shadows.

Luke studied the tightrope again. There was no net below, and a fall from this height would definitely kill him. Nobody was going to make him step out onto the high wire. But he had to do it.

Using the methods of relaxation and control he had learned, first from Obi-Wan Kenobi, whom everyone had called Ben, and later from Yoda the Jedi Master, Luke calmed himself. He had not yet finished his schooling. He remembered his confrontation with Darth Vader, when

Vader had claimed to be his father. It couldn't be true! But what if it *was*?

Luke pushed the thought away. He could not dwell on it now. He had to master his Jedi skills before he could do himself, or anyone else, any good. He had to trust in the Force and move on. He reached out for the energy of the Force, warm and bright, and wrapped himself in it like a suit of armor. Once again, the Force was there for him.

But something else was there, too, pulling at him from the shadows, just out of reach; a hard, powerful coldness that was the opposite of what his teachers had shown him. It was the part of the Force that gave Darth Vader such power.

The dark side.

No! Luke thought, pushing the dark side away. He took a deep breath, drew the brightness of the Force around him again, and stepped out onto the wire. Suddenly it was effortless, as though the wire had become as wide as a public sidewalk.

Halfway across the wire, he started to run. He told himself it was part of the test. He told himself that the Force was with him, that he could rise above his father's fall to the dark side, that anything was possible to one trained as a Jedi Knight.

He tried not to believe that he ran because he could feel the dark side walking the wire behind him, its evil tracking his every step. Following him . . . and gaining.

———

Xizor sat in the semidarkened room, watching a holoprojection of various assassins-for-hire, trying to decide whether to employ them or not. The candidates were presented by Guri, his bodyguard and confidante.

"Hire them," Xizor said, happy with Guri's latest candidates, and Guri left to fulfill his order.

Guri looked like an extremely beautiful human woman. But Guri wasn't human. She was an HRD, a human replica droid. They were rare to begin with, but Guri was the only HRD in existence programmed to be an assassin. She had cost Xizor nine million credits but was worth every one. He had billions of credits anyway. They weren't important.

Only power was important.

Xizor was of the Falleen, a species whose distant ancestors had been reptiles, and who had evolved into what was generally considered the most beautiful of all humanoid races. He was over a hundred years old, but he looked thirty. He was tall and handsome, with a topknot ponytail jutting up from his otherwise bald head. He also exuded natural aromas that made most human-stock females feel instantly attracted to him. He could kick a sunfruit off the top of a tall humanoid's head with little effort and was strong enough to lift twice his weight over his head without breaking a sweat. But that was not the kind of power he cared about.

Xizor was the third most powerful being in the galaxy. Only the Emperor and Darth Vader had more power than he. But if his plans went as he hoped, he was about to move up in the ranks. Months had passed since he had overheard the Emperor and Vader talking of Luke Skywalker. Xizor had spent that time plotting, and now he was ready to put his plans into motion.

One hour to go before his meeting.

Xizor waited patiently as the minutes slipped by. After a while he rose. Time to go and see Vader. By going there instead of insisting that Vader come to him, he would seem to be putting himself at a disadvantage. It didn't matter. That was part of the plan; no one must suspect that he felt anything but the greatest respect for Darth Vader, not if Xizor's plans were going to succeed. And he was sure they would.

They always did.

Leia sat in a nasty bar in the bad part of Mos Eisley. The place was hot, the desert air outside seeping in along with the riffraff that came to hang out there.

She decided that Lando Calrissian had picked this bar on purpose just to bug her. Leia had hated Lando for a time, until she had finally understood that when he had betrayed Han on Cloud City, it had been part of his plan to save them from Darth Vader. Lando had given up a lot for that, and they all owed him for it.

Leia was glad Chewbacca was sitting next to her, snarling if any of the other customers came too close. The only reason Chewie had left her with Luke after the last meeting with Vader was so that he could go with Lando to Tatooine and set up Han's rescue. Once Leia had arrived, Chewie had been with her constantly. As far as Leia knew, Chewbacca intended to be her bodyguard as long as he was alive, or until Han was rescued.

"Buy you a drink, beautiful?" somebody said behind her.

Leia turned. It was Lando. She was angry at him but glad to see him, too. "How'd you get in here?" she asked.

"Back door," Lando said. He smiled. He was a handsome man, and he knew it.

Behind him were the droids R2-D2 and C-3PO. Artoo's dome swiveled as the droid looked around the bar. Threepio managed to look nervous, even though he could not change his facial expression.

Artoo whistled.

"Yes, I see that," Threepio said. A short pause. "Master Lando, wouldn't it be better if we waited outside? I don't think they like droids in this place. We're the only ones here."

"Relax," Lando said with a smile. "Nobody is going to bother you. I know the owner.

"Listen, Leia," Lando continued, very serious now. "I think we've finally tracked Boba Fett's ship."

Hope sprang up in Leia's heart. Boba Fett was the bounty hunter who had taken Han Solo, frozen in carbonite, from Cloud City. Boba Fett was to turn Han over to his employer, the criminal called Jabba the Hutt, here on Tatooine. Chances were, if they found Boba Fett, they would find Han, and never have to go up against Jabba at all. The problem was, Boba Fett had not yet reached Tatooine.

"Where is he?" Leia asked.

11

"A moon called Gall in one of the far Rim systems. An old gambling buddy of mine named Dash Rendar is checking it out for us," Lando said.

"Fine. How soon will we know?" Leia asked.

"A few days," Lando answered.

"Anything would be better than waiting here," Leia said, looking around in disgust.

"Gall is controlled by the Empire," Lando said worriedly. "There are two Imperial Star Destroyers stationed there, plus a number of TIE fighters. If Fett's ship is there, it won't be easy to get to him."

"When has anything been easy since I met you?" Leia asked.

For once Lando didn't have an answer.

Xizor left his four bodyguards in the outer room and went into Darth Vader's personal meeting chamber. The guards were trained in half a dozen forms of hand-to-hand combat, each armed with a blaster and each an expert shot; still, if Vader wanted to harm him, it wouldn't matter if he took four men or forty with him. The mysterious Force would let Vader block a fired blaster bolt with his lightsaber or his hands, and he could kill with a gesture. He could freeze your lungs or stop your heart, just like that. It was a lesson many had learned the hard way: One did not stand toe to toe with Darth Vader and challenge him directly.

Fortunately, Xizor had the Emperor's goodwill. As long as that was the case, Vader would not dare harm him.

The meeting room was very plain. There were chairs, a

table, and a hologram projector. There were no signs of Vader's great wealth, which was almost as great as Xizor's own. Like the Dark Prince, Vader cared little for wealth itself.

The wall at the opposite end of the room slid open silently, and Vader stood there. He looked quite dramatic in his cape and black uniform. Xizor could hear his breathing inside the armored helmet and mask.

Xizor stood and bowed. "You asked to see me, Lord Vader," he began. "How may I be of service to you?"

As he stepped into the room, Vader said, "My master bids me to arrange for a fleet of your cargo ships to deliver supplies to our bases on the Rim."

"But of course," Xizor said. "My entire operation is at your disposal; I am always happy to aid the Empire in any way that I can."

Xizor was a criminal. But he also ran legal businesses, including Xizor Transport Systems, a shipping company commonly referred to as XTS.

The two beings pretended to respect one another, but every conversation they had was a contest to see which one would come out on top. Xizor had no doubt that Vader looked upon him as a potential enemy. Xizor considered Vader a mortal enemy, perhaps his greatest foe.

Ten years earlier, Vader had been in charge of a military research lab on Xizor's homeworld of Falleen. An experimental virus was accidentally released and became a plague. To stop the whole planet from falling to the plague, Vader had ordered the entire city around the lab destroyed. Two hundred thousand people, including

Xizor's mother, father, brother, two sisters, and three uncles, had been killed by lasers fired on the city from orbit around the planet. Xizor had been offworld at the time. Otherwise he would have been just another victim.

The Empire, and Vader, had destroyed all those lives to save several billion others. To them it had been a small price to pay to prevent the plague from spreading. To Xizor it was another matter entirely.

He had never spoken of the tragedy. He'd had his family's deaths erased from Imperial records. Nobody knew that Xizor the Dark Prince had personal reasons to hate Darth Vader. Xizor had been patient, knowing that his revenge was only a matter of time. Now, at last, the time was almost at hand. He would remove Vader, not only as an obstacle preventing him from gaining more power, but also as the murderer of his family.

But he would not kill Vader. That would be too merciful, and dangerous as well. To live in disgrace would be a much more terrible fate for Vader. To be abandoned by the Emperor would destroy him. That was justice.

"We shall need three hundred ships," Vader said, cutting into Xizor's thoughts. "Half of them tankers, half dry cargo transports. Standard Imperial delivery contracts. There is a large . . . *construction* project of which you are aware. Can you supply the vessels?"

"Yes, my lord," Xizor answered. "Just tell me where and when you desire them and I will make it so. And Imperial terms are acceptable."

Vader stood silently for a moment, the only sound the mechanical wheeze of his breathing.

He didn't expect that, Xizor thought. *He thought I might argue or try to haggle over the price. Good.*

"Very well," Vader finally said. "I'll have the fleet supply admiral contact you with details."

"It is my honor to serve," Xizor said. Again he gave Vader a military bow, a bit lower and slower than before.

Without another word, Vader turned. The wall slid back again, and he swept from the room. Anybody watching would see that Vader's behavior was almost rude in comparison to Xizor's.

Xizor allowed himself a tiny smile.

Everything was going according to plan.

2

Inside what had once been Ben Kenobi's home, Luke took a break from working on his new lightsaber. The old place was on the edge of the Western Dune Sea. It was sturdy and good protection against the sandstorms. Luke was thinking of Ben, who had been struck down by Vader on the Death Star.

Suddenly he felt something.

It was like hearing and smelling and tasting and seeing somehow combined, and yet it was none of those things. Something . . . coming, somehow.

Whatever it was grew stronger. For a moment he had a flash of recognition: Leia?

He had been able to call to her when he was about to fall from beneath Cloud City after his encounter with Vader. She had somehow received his cry for help.

He buckled on his blaster and went outside. Once he got the lightsaber built and working, he hoped he would be able to put the blaster away. A true Jedi did not need any other weapon to protect himself, Ben had told him.

Luke sighed. He had a way to go to get to that level.

A hot wind blew grit off the desert, scraping and drying

his skin. In the distance, he saw a thin dust cloud. Somebody was coming across the desert from Mos Eisley.

In his most private chamber, the Emperor sat staring at a life-size holographic recording: Prince Xizor choking a man who'd attempted to murder him in one of Imperial Center's high-security protected corridors. The man had not stood a chance. The Emperor smiled and turned in his floating chair to look at Darth Vader.

"Well," the Emperor said, "it seems that Prince Xizor has kept up his martial arts practice, does it not?"

Vader frowned. "He is a dangerous man, my master. Not to be trusted."

The Emperor favored him with one of his unattractive, toothy smiles. "Do not trouble yourself with Xizor, Lord Vader. He is my concern."

"As you wish," Vader said, and bowed.

"One wonders how the assassin managed to get into a protected corridor," the Emperor said. But there was no wonder in the Emperor's voice.

Vader froze. The Emperor knew. No one else could have known Vader was involved, since Vader himself had eliminated the guard who had admitted Xizor's would-be killer into the corridor. But somehow, the Emperor knew.

The Emperor's mastery of the dark side was great indeed.

"I will look into it, my master," Vader said.

"Don't bother," the Emperor answered. "There was no harm done. Though I would hate to see anything happen to him as long as he is useful."

Vader bowed again. The Emperor had made his point. Vader would make no further attempts to test Xizor's ability to defend himself against deadly attack.

Not yet, anyway.

As the landspeeder carrying them neared their destination, Leia saw Luke standing next to the house, watching. He must have sensed them coming, through the Force, she realized. The power of the Force amazed her.

Chewie brought the speeder to a stop. Dust kicked up by the repulsors floated around them for a moment before the lashing winds swirled it away.

"Hey, Luke," Lando said.

Chewie added what had to be a greeting.

"Master Luke, it's so good to see you again," Threepio said.

Even Artoo whistled a happy greeting.

They all liked Luke. There was just something about him. Maybe it was the Force flowing through him. Maybe it was just because he seemed so . . . good.

"Come on inside," Luke said, smiling warmly.

When they told Luke why they'd come, he was immediately excited. He was ready to hop into his X-wing and leave.

"Hold on a second," Lando said. "First we have to make sure Fett's there. Then there's the little matter of the Imperial Navy."

"Hey, we can fly circles around those guys," Luke said with a shrug.

Chewie spoke up.

Threepio translated: "Ah, Chewbacca wonders if perhaps the Rebel Alliance might not be willing to help, given Master Han's services to them."

Luke grinned like a child seeing a new toy. "Sure they would. Wedge is in command of the Rogue Squadron now, and he told me if I ever needed them they'd come running."

"They can drop whatever they're doing, just like that?" Lando asked.

"I don't see why not," Leia said. "Rogue Squadron doesn't have any permanent assignment, and I'm sure I can convince the Alliance that Captain Solo is worth rescuing."

"Great," Luke said. "Let's do it!"

"I've got the *Millennium Falcon* ready to go," Lando said. "How long will it take you to get your X-wing operational?"

"I'll meet you in orbit," Luke said. He grinned. The waiting was over.

Leia said, "I'll get off a coded call to Rogue Squadron." Luke nodded.

They were going to get Han.

"Have you assembled all the information on Skywalker?" Xizor asked.

"Yes, my prince," Guri answered.

Xizor stared into space. His organization was huge, the people working for him numbering in the tens of thousands, but some things he had to deal with personally. Especially something as sensitive as the Skywalker situation.

"All of the material has been checked and rechecked?" he asked.

"As you ordered," she said.

"Very well," he said, and nodded. "Unleash the bounty hunters and assassins."

Vader wanted Skywalker, wanted him alive to give to the Emperor.

Black Sun's reach was long and wide, and what information there was on Skywalker was now in Xizor's personal computer system. Skywalker, who apparently considered himself a Jedi Knight—though the Jedi were supposed to be extinct—had participated in the Rebel raid on the Death Star months ago. His closest allies were Princess Leia Organa, once of Alderaan, a Wookiee called Chewbacca, and Han Solo, a notorious smuggler-turned-Rebel.

Solo had been handed over to a bounty hunter called Boba Fett after a confrontation on Cloud City. Fett was to deliver Solo to the crime boss known as Jabba the Hutt, on Tatooine, but had not yet arrived there. Skywalker would try to rescue his friend Captain Solo from Fett. The problem was, Xizor did not know where Fett was.

Darth Vader had all but promised to deliver Skywalker alive to the Emperor. If Vader should fail in his promise . . . well, things would not go well for Vader.

In the end, Xizor knew he had found the perfect weapon with which to finally defeat Darth Vader.

The death of Luke Skywalker.

"Put out the information that those seeking to claim the reward for Skywalker would be advised to locate the bounty hunter Boba Fett," he commanded. "Sooner or later, Skywalker will go after Fett."

Xizor smiled.

"Then we will have him."

3

The *Millennium Falcon* and Luke's X-wing fighter dropped out of hyperspace not far from one another. Luke kept the little ship close to the *Falcon* as they neared the moon Gall. Rogue Squadron appeared on his scope about the time he got the call over his comm.

"Hey, Luke! Welcome to the end of the galaxy!"

"Hey, Wedge! How's it going, buddy?" Luke called.

"So-so. Another day, another credit—before taxes, of course," Wedge replied with a laugh.

Luke smiled. Wedge Antilles was one of the Alliance pilots who had survived the attack on the Death Star. He could fly, and he was braver than he had any right to be. Good old Wedge. A moment later Luke spotted Rogue Squadron off to his right.

"Follow us, Luke," Wedge said. "We've got camp set up on a little moon called Kile in the planet shadow opposite Gall. We've fixed it up real nice—air, gravity, water, all the comforts of home."

"Lead on," Luke said. "We're right behind you."

"You call this 'real nice'?" Leia said as she looked around inside the prefab building the Rogue Squadron had set up as a base. It was basically four walls and a roof and looked like a cross between a warehouse and a hangar. "I'd hate to see a place you thought wasn't real nice."

Wedge led them to a corner of the building where a table and a holoprojector unit had been set up. A man sat sprawled in a chair, looking as if he were asleep. Though he had red hair and pale skin, something about the way he sat reminded Leia of Han.

Suddenly his eyes flicked open, and he was on his feet before they reached him. He was tall and lean, with shining green eyes, and he wore his blaster low on his hip. He made a low, theatrical bow.

"Princess Leia," he said. "How delightful of you to visit us here in our humble castle, Your Highness." He waved at the big, empty room and grinned.

Leia shook her head. Now he really reminded her of Han. She wondered if all these space adventurer types took lessons in how to be wise guys.

"This is my informant, Dash Rendar," Lando said, "thief, card cheat, smuggler, and an okay pilot."

"What do you mean 'okay pilot,' Calrissian?" Dash asked, his grin growing wider. "I can fly rings around you."

"And you're modest, too," Leia said.

Dash bowed low. "I see that the princess has a keen eye to go with her stunning beauty."

Oh, brother, Leia thought. *This guy is going to lead us to Boba Fett?*

"How's the mission plan coming?" Luke asked Wedge.

"We've done a little recon work, couple of flybys,"

Wedge said, moving to the holoprojector. "Let me show you the layout."

Wedge began showing them the holographic maps and recorded images of the moon where Boba Fett's ship was supposed to be docked. The Imperial Enclave on Gall was home base to two Star Destroyers. A standard Destroyer carried seventy-two TIE fighters. A hundred and forty-four of them against the twelve in the Rogue Squadron. Thirteen, counting Luke's ship. That made the odds a hair less than twelve to one. Not so bad compared to some battles they'd been in.

"That's about it," Wedge finally said. "What do you think, Luke?"

"Piece of cake," Luke said. "I know just how to do it."

Leia and Lando both looked at him as if he'd turned into a giant spider. He grinned again and explained his plan.

"That's it?" Leia laughed.

"What's wrong with it?" Luke asked.

"You and the Rogue Squadron will attack the Imperial Enclave, keep a hundred-and-some-odd TIE fighters and two Star Destroyers busy while Dash leads the *Millennium Falcon* to where Boba Fett's ship is docked? We'll just land, rescue Han, and fly away? Why, nothing is wrong with that plan. What could possibly be wrong? It's perfect!" Leia shook her head in distress.

"Okay, so it's simple—" Luke began.

"Simpleminded," Leia said.

He set his jaw. Uh-oh. She'd insulted him. She knew that look.

"If you have a better idea . . . ?" Luke said, his voice tight.

Leia sighed. That was the problem. She didn't have a better idea.

"Not to put a damper on things," Dash said, "but if we're going to sneak in the back way, it'll take some pretty fancy flying. Think you can handle it?" he asked Lando.

"Hey," Lando said. "If a guy like you can do it, a respectable gentleman such as myself should have no problem."

Everyone smiled, but Luke did not feel as confident as the others. Sure, it was his plan. And he knew it would work. The problem was, they were counting on Dash Rendar an awful lot, both for information and to live up to his bragging as a pilot. Lando seemed to think they could trust Dash as long as he was paid.

Luke wasn't so sure.

"This is Rogue Leader," Luke said. "Lock into attack position."

Rogue Squadron acknowledged Luke's orders. They were as ready as they were going to get. One of the pair of Destroyers lay dead ahead.

A score of TIE fighters spewed from the Destroyer's flight bay ports.

"Here they come," Rogue Six said. That was Wes Janson, an old hand.

"I see them, Wes," Luke said. "Everybody stay alert! Attack speed, take out whatever's in your scope."

"Yeeehhaaawww!" one of the squad yelled into the comm.

Luke had to smile. He really should tell whoever it was—sounded like Rogue Five, that was Dix—to bottle the unofficial commspeak, but he knew just how the pilot felt.

"Watch yourselves," Luke said.

Then the battle began.

On the *Millennium Falcon*, Leia crouched down behind Chewie and Lando in the control cockpit. Threepio stood in the doorway behind them.

"Do be careful, Master Lando. We're awfully close to the tops of those trees!"

"Oh, really?" Lando said. "I hadn't noticed."

Ahead of them a couple of hundred meters, Dash flew his ship, the *Outrider,* and the wind of his passage was enough to fan the tall evergreens below. The ship cleared the treetops by no more than five meters.

"Any closer and we'll get green stains on our belly," Leia said.

"Tell me about it," Lando said. "He said we'd have to fly low, but I didn't realize he meant this low."

"What's with this guy?" Leia asked. "What's he trying to prove?"

"You never heard the story of the Rendars?" Lando asked.

"Should I have?"

"Dash was at the Imperial Star Academy, a year or so behind Han. His family was wealthy. Dash's older brother was a freighter pilot working his way up through the family shipping company. There was an accident, not the pilot's fault, and the freighter crashed on Imperial Center. Killed the crew, destroyed the ship."

"Terrible," Leia said. "But I don't—"

"The freighter hit the Emperor's private museum. Place had a lot of his mementos in it; most were lost in the fire caused by the crash. The Emperor wasn't happy. He had the Rendar family's property seized, then banished them from Imperial Center. Including Dash. He was forced out of the Academy."

"Well, then, why isn't he working for the Alliance with the rest of us?" Leia asked.

"He works for whoever pays the most," Lando said. "He's downright magic with anything that flies, and a good shot with a blaster. He's a good man to have at your back when the going gets hot—as long as your money lasts."

Four TIE fighters roared in.

Luke yelled at Wedge. "Rogue One, look out! On your port, bearing three-oh-five!"

Wedge's X-wing immediately peeled left and down. "Thanks, Luke!"

Luke punched it, swung a shallow turn, and headed straight for the attacking squad.

Use the Force, Luke.

Luke grinned. The first time he'd heard that, during the

attack on the Death Star, he hadn't understood. He knew what it meant now.

"Targeting sensors off, rear shields off, reroute more power to the guns," he ordered.

Artoo was not pleased and said so.

"Sorry, buddy, but this way is better."

Luke reached out. The Force was there, and he let it fill him. The TIE fighters suddenly seemed to be moving more slowly. Luke's hands flew over the controls. Lines of fire lanced out and shattered two of the four TIE fighters.

"Fine shootin', Rogue Leader," Rogue Five said.

"Thanks, Dix," Luke responded.

"Six more coming in," Rogue Four said.

The X-wings and TIE fighters streaked back and forth through the blackness of space, blasting at each other. Twelve more TIEs appeared on Luke's scope. The odds were getting worse.

4

Luke kept the Rogues spiraling in and out, to keep the Destroyer's big guns from locking on them. They were doing okay so far.

"Look out, Dixie!" Wedge yelled.

Luke saw the danger. A TIE fighter had gotten below Dix and now bore in, firing at the X-wing's exposed belly. Dix cut hard to his right.

Too late. The deadly lasers raked the X-wing like fiery claws. Dix's ship blew apart in a fireball, leaving nothing but blasted wreckage.

Luke felt his stomach turn. They'd lost Dix.

Suddenly it wasn't a game. People were dying. Good people. He could never lose sight of that, not for a moment. It was only fun as long as nobody got hurt, and that part never lasted.

Now it got worse. The second Destroyer appeared and began unloading its fighters. No more time to think, no time to worry. Luke abandoned himself to the Force.

Rogue Squadron was outmatched. Lando, Leia, and the others had probably made it to the shipyard already. Luke and the Rogues had done their job. It was time to go.

"Okay, Rogue Squadron," Luke said. "We're out of here."

"There it is, dead ahead," Dash said.

The lights of the shipyard blazed in the darkness.

Leia leaned forward. Strained to see . . .

"There it is! There's Fett's ship!"

"Been fun, people," Dash said. "See you around."

Ahead of them, the *Outrider* pulled up in a hard climb and rocketed toward space.

"Where are you going?" Lando shouted.

"Hey, you didn't pay me to shoot, only to guide. I'm outta here."

"Dash, blast you!" Lando barked.

"Never mind," Leia put in quickly. "We don't need him."

Chewie pointed at the sensor screen and said something.

"Oh, dear!" Threepio said.

"I wish you'd stop saying that," Leia snapped. "What?"

Lando spoke before the droid could. "Company. We've got half a dozen TIE fighters on our tail!"

"Is that all?" Leia asked. "For a hotshot pilot like you, that shouldn't be a problem, right?"

"Yeah, right," Lando said, and nodded. "But just for fun, why don't you and Chewie go see if the guns still work?"

Now things were really going to get interesting.

———

The Rogue Squadron peeled away from the engagement.

The TIE fighters, who'd obviously been ordered to defend but not to pursue, allowed them to go. Most of them.

As the Rogues sped from the battle, Luke felt a sudden wave of something he couldn't quite identify wash over him. Like a sense of danger that couldn't be ignored, some kind of warning.

Luke!

Obi-Wan!

He jerked the control stick between his knees to the side without questioning further.

The beam from a laser cannon flashed past.

If he hadn't moved it would have cooked him.

But there weren't any TIEs behind him! Only Rogue Six. As he watched, Wes's X-wing altered course to follow him. What—?

"Wes! What are you doing?"

Wes shouted, "Luke! Something's gone wrong with my R2 unit! It's taken control of my ship! My stick is dead!"

Yeah, Luke thought, *I'll be dead, too, if I don't do something.*

Luke pulled the stick back into his belly and hit full thrust. The X-wing responded; acceleration mashed him into the seat, his face stretched and flattened as if a giant hand was pressing hard fingers against the skin and muscles.

"Everybody get clear!" Luke managed to say through peeled-back lips. What was going on? He'd almost been fried by one of his own! Behind him, Wes's X-wing copied Luke's maneuver, trying to stay with him.

This was bad, this was very bad. What was he going to do? Sooner or later the out-of-control X-wing would blast him.

He dodged another blast and looped around behind Wes. Then he fired, realizing that a mistake could cost Wes his life. His blast cut through the runaway X-wing's main engine, killing it. Rogue Six's thrusters flamed out. It couldn't fly very well, but it could still shoot.

"More of those TIEs coming back, Luke," somebody said.

"Not now!" he cursed. Once again he let the Force direct his aim, gave himself to it. He pinpointed Rogue Six's weapons control system and fired.

A hit!

Now Wes's guns were dead and he—or his crazed droid—couldn't fire the lasers or the belly missiles.

He sighed. *Thank goodness.* What in the galaxy could have caused it to malfunction that way?

"Hey, I'm sorry, Luke, I don't know what happened!" Wes said over the comlink.

"Don't worry about it. Wedge will tow you back with a magnetic line. Let's get out of here."

"Copy that, Luke."

Leia fired the *Falcon's* belly guns at the incoming TIE fighter. The Imperial craft flew right into the beams. Exploded. That was three she'd gotten, and Chewie had hit some of them, too, but more were swarming in.

Too many more.

"We can't land," Lando said over the comm. "If we put it down on the deck, we'll get blasted!"

"What are we going to do?" Leia said.

"I don't know," he answered. "We can't keep flying around—uh-oh."

" 'Uh-oh' what?" Leia asked in alarm.

"Boba Fett's ship—it's taking off." Lando cursed.

"Follow it!" Leia ordered.

"How? There's a wall of Imperial fighters between it and us!"

"Go around them!" she cried.

She was too close to lose Han now.

"I'll try," Lando promised.

The *Falcon* dove, bottomed out, and then Lando hit the throttles hard in a climbing turn. Another TIE fighter came into view. Leia started the guns working, but the fighter zipped past, too fast. *Missed it.* She felt the *Falcon* rock as the shields were hit by enemy fire. Her gun beams lanced out and pierced one of the fighters, sent it spinning away, riddled with holes.

She missed the other one. Chewie yelled something, and she wished she could understand his language.

"I hate to be the one to say it," Lando said, "but I have a bad feeling about this."

Back at Rogue Squadron's secret moonbase, Luke and Wedge hurried from their fighters to where Wes's X-wing had been towed. Wes stood there staring at his ruined ship.

"You all right?" Luke asked Wes.

"Yeah, I'm fine," Wes said with a shrug. "I'd sure like to know what my R2 unit ate for breakfast, though. What could have gotten into it?"

"Why don't we see if we can find out?" Luke said, then turned to the crew chief and added, "Get a coupler on this R2 unit, would you?"

As the malfunctioning R2 unit was settled to the ground, the crew chief stepped in and stuck a restraining bolt on it before it could move. Artoo-Detoo moved closer, extruded an interface and plugged into the other R2 unit.

Artoo whistled frantically.

"Uh-oh," Luke said, looking at the translation screen.

"What?" Wedge said.

"Artoo says the droid wasn't malfunctioning. He says it was programmed to shoot at me."

Wedge whistled. "Who would do that?"

The chief pulled her comlink from her belt and spoke into it, then listened. Luke couldn't hear who was on the other end.

"That's Rendar coming in," the chief said.

"What about Leia and Lando?" Luke asked.

The chief shrugged. "He didn't say."

"Keep an eye on this droid, Chief. Don't let anybody touch it," Luke said. "Wedge, come with me."

Luke hurried to the second hangar, where Dash's ship would arrive shortly.

––––––

The *Falcon* arced away from the shipyard and dived between two half-constructed towers. Leia saw that they were outrunning their pursuers.

"What are you doing?" Leia asked over the comm.

"Saving our lives," Lando said. "I used every trick in the manual, plus a few I made up, and I couldn't get past those fighters. There were too many of them. It was just a matter of time before they knocked us down."

"What about Boba Fett?" she asked.

"I lost sight of him," he admitted.

"He's probably already in hyperspace," she said, frustrated.

Chewie said something.

"Chewbacca is right," Threepio said. "Sooner or later Master Han will be delivered to Jabba. We can always go back to Tatooine and wait. I think that is a very good idea."

Nobody spoke.

Threepio continued, "Well, at least we're alive."

Luke almost took a swing at Dash. It was all he could do to restrain himself.

"Easy, Luke," Wedge cautioned.

Dash stood there, looking relaxed, and shrugged.

"You just left them there?" Luke asked again.

"Hey, kid, I was paid to show them where Fett's ship was. I did that. My job was done. If they'd wanted me to do anything else, they should have contracted for it up front," Dash said.

"If anything happens to them . . . ," Luke said, the warning clear in his tone.

"What, kid?" Dash asked, lifting one eyebrow. "You gonna shoot me? I was hired as a guide, and I guided. End of story."

One of the hangar crew ran over to where they stood.

"We've just heard from Calrissian," the man said. "They're about fifteen minutes out."

Luke was relieved. They were all right.

"That gives us a few minutes," Wedge said. "Let's go and see what we can dig out of that trashed R2 unit."

"Good idea," Luke agreed.

But when they reached the place where the droid had been, what they found was a smoldering pile of debris.

Somebody had blasted the droid into rubble.

Luke spun around, looking for the crew chief who was supposed to be watching the unit. He spotted the woman quickly enough.

She was pointing a blaster right at him.

5

L uke saw Wedge reach for his blaster.

"No!" he yelled.

Too late.

The chief saw Wedge go for his weapon, turned slightly, and shot at him. The blast sizzled between Luke and Wedge, missing Luke by centimeters.

Wedge didn't have any choice. His blaster beam caught the chief squarely in the chest and knocked her sprawling.

By the time Luke got to her, the chief wasn't going to be answering any questions ever again.

"Well, I guess we know who programmed the droid to kill me," Luke said, his voice quiet. "I would have liked to know why."

Wedge shook his head. "Maybe we can find out. I'll see what the operations computer has on her."

A few minutes later the *Millennium Falcon* landed. When Luke saw Leia, he was immediately concerned. She looked terrible. She walked as if she were a thousand years old. Luke hugged her, but she was limp in his arms.

"What happened?" he asked.

"Boba Fett got away," she said.

Behind them Lando said, "Yeah, and we were lucky to

get away ourselves. The place was thick with TIE fighters. I'm sorry, Luke. I tried."

Luke nodded. He turned, one arm still around Leia.

"Come on," he said to her. "We'll figure something else out."

Leia was depressed, but the news of the malfunctioning droid frightened her. When Wedge and Lando came back from checking on the former crew chief through the opcom, they looked grim.

"What?" she asked.

"Well," Wedge said, "it seems there was a transfer for ten thousand credits into the chief's account a few days ago, just after Rogue Squadron arrived here."

"The money came from a dummy corporation," Lando said. "I managed to backwalk it through two more dummy corporations. Wound up with something called Saber Enterprises. Last I heard, Saber was a front organization for the Empire's secret undercover antiespionage operation."

"It's got Vader's gloveprints all over it," Leia said.

"That doesn't make any sense," Luke replied, shaking his head.

"Why not?" Leia asked.

"He wants me alive," Luke said. "He wants me to join the Empire."

"Maybe he changed his mind," Lando said.

Leia stared off into the distance. This was bad. She'd lost Han, maybe forever, and she didn't want to lose

38

Luke, too. He was too important, not just to the Alliance, but to her.

She loved Han, but she loved Luke, too. Maybe not in the same way, but she didn't want to see him hurt. This attempt on Luke's life was just the tip of something much larger.

She had to find out what it was and stop it.

"The first attempt on Skywalker's life has failed," Guri announced to Xizor. "The bribed crew chief is dead."

"No surprise." Xizor shrugged. "We knew the boy was extremely lucky. In any case, allow our agents to proceed. Be certain it looks as if they are in the employ of the Empire, linked directly to Vader. If they get Skywalker, good. If not, I have another idea that might be even better for us."

"As you wish," she answered.

"Before you leave, put in a comm to Darth Vader. I would like to see him at his convenience."

"Yes, my prince," she said.

"That will be all," Xizor said, and waved her away.

Darth Vader stared at the hologram of Xizor's human replica droid.

"Very well, Guri," he said. "Tell your master I will see him. Have him meet me on the Emperor's skyhook in three hours."

Vader broke the connection. What did Xizor want? Whatever it was, he did not believe for a moment that it was to serve the Empire—unless it served Xizor first. Vader ordered that his personal shuttle be prepared to fly to the skyhook, a giant orbiting satellite.

As he waited for the shuttle to be prepared, he considered another problem. For the moment, the Emperor did not wish him to seek out Luke Skywalker personally. There were other obligations he must see to first.

Very well. He could not seek Luke out in person, but he could arrange for others to do so. A very large reward and the gratitude of Darth Vader had been offered to whoever brought Skywalker to him alive. That would have to do for now.

"Why me?" Luke asked.

"Because Tatooine is your homeworld and you're the most familiar with it," Leia said. "Somebody needs to be there to keep an eye out for Boba Fett. You're the logical choice."

Luke shook his head. He didn't like it.

"Can't your Alliance business wait?" he asked.

"No. Take Artoo and go back to Ben's house. Lando and Chewie and Threepio and I will meet you there as soon as I am done."

Luke sighed. "All right. But you be careful."

After Luke was gone, Leia spoke to Dash Rendar.

"Are you available for a job?" she asked him.

"Sweetie," he answered, "I'm always available if the money is right."

"I want you to go to Tatooine and keep an eye on Luke," she said.

Dash raised an eyebrow. "Bodyguard? Sure, I can do that. Kid won't like it if he finds out."

"So stay out of sight," Leia said. "Somebody tried to kill him, and I think they'll try again. How much?"

Dash named a figure.

Lando whistled. "Man, you are a bandit, aren't you?" he said.

"The best don't come cheap," Dash said with a grin.

After she'd paid Dash and he was gone, Leia took Lando aside. "What would be the best way to contact somebody high up in Black Sun?"

Lando stared at her as if she'd just told him she could fly by waving her arms. He shook his head. "The best way? Don't."

"Come on, Lando. This is important."

"Princess, Black Sun is bad news," Lando said.

"Somebody just tried to kill Luke," Leia replied calmly. "Maybe it was Vader. Maybe not. Black Sun has a vast spynet. It is older, and maybe even wider than the Alliance's. They can find out who is responsible."

Chewie half grunted, half moaned something.

"I'm with you, pal," Lando said, then exchanged glances with Chewie. "This is a big mistake."

Leia continued, "But you have the connections and can put me in touch with them, right?"

"It's still a bad idea," Lando repeated.

"Lando . . ."

"Yeah, yeah. I know a few people," he said finally, giving in.

She smiled. "Good. Where do we find them?"

On a balcony overlooking a garden aboard the Emperor's skyhook, Xizor waited for Darth Vader. He felt Vader approach before he heard or saw him. Xizor turned and offered a small bow. "Lord Vader."

"Prince Xizor," Vader answered. "You had something to discuss?"

"Yes," Xizor answered. "The location of a secret Rebel base has come to my attention. I assumed you would want to know of this."

Vader was silent except for his measured, mechanical breathing, which suddenly seemed quite loud.

"Of course," Vader finally said. "Where is this base?"

"In the Baji Sector, out on the Rim," Xizor said. "It is my understanding that there is a shipyard full of vessels undergoing repair. There are hundreds of Rebel ships, ranging from fighters to troop carriers. Destruction of such a base would no doubt cripple the Alliance."

"I'll have my agents look into this," Vader said. "If it is as you say, then the Empire will be indebted to you."

Xizor gave Vader a courteous nod. "Merely my duty, Lord Vader. No thanks are necessary."

Xizor knew that the Emperor would be very appreciative. He would probably send Vader to destroy the base. That would get Vader out of the way and allow Xizor a bit more freedom to continue the unfolding of his plan.

———

"So our agents have verified this report?" the Emperor asked Vader.

"They have, my master," Vader answered.

"A hundred Rebel ships? Plus, no doubt, their pilots and officers."

"Likely, yes," Vader agreed.

"Well. You must take part of the fleet and go there immediately. Destroy the base," the Emperor ordered. "The loss of ships and troops will be most damaging to the Rebels."

"I thought perhaps Admiral Okins might command the expedition," Vader suggested.

The Emperor smiled. "Did you?"

Vader felt his hope evaporate. "But if it is your wish, I shall lead the attack."

"It is my wish. You may take Okins if you like, but you are to personally ensure the assault."

Vader bowed. "Yes, my master."

As he left the Emperor's private chamber, Vader fumed. The base was there, just as Xizor had said. It would be a powerful victory for the Empire and relatively easy. Ships under repair would not be able to fly to defend themselves. But Vader did not trust the Dark Prince, and he knew the Falleen did nothing for free.

What was in this for Xizor? What did he hope to gain?

6

Luke took a deep breath. He stood outside Ben's house on Tatooine, the first stars of evening aglimmer, the moon still on the rise. The air was warm but not as scorchingly hot as it had been. He had completed his lightsaber and now held it in his right hand, hoping it would work. He'd come outside to test it. That way, if it blew up, at least it wouldn't take Ben's house with it.

Luke took another deep breath and pushed the control button. The lightsaber glowed, the blade extruded to full length, just under a meter, and began to hum with power. It gave off a green gleam that was bright in the early dark.

Luke grinned.

Well, it wasn't as if he'd really thought it was going to explode.

He waved the lightsaber experimentally. It had a good balance, maybe even better than his first one. He drew himself up into a ready stance, slid forward, and swung through a series of downward cuts, alternating from left to right.

Yes!

Maybe he would learn how to be a Jedi Knight after all.

Leia, Chewie, and Lando sat in the private office of a casino owner on the planet Rodia. The owner's name was Avaro. His skin had faded to a dull green, he was much fatter than most of the Rodians Leia had seen, and he spoke with a lisping accent.

"So you will put us in touch with Black Sun?" she asked.

Avaro nodded. "Yeth. It will take a few dayth. Local contakth won't do you any good, you need an offplanet wepwethentative."

"Fine."

"Meanwhile, feel fwee to enjoy owah cathino," Avaro added. "Wooms will be made available fowah you."

Leia nodded. "Thanks."

If Mos Eisley was bad, this place was worse, Leia thought, as they left Avaro's office and moved toward the hotel section of the casino. There were electronic gambling devices, card games, wheels of fortune, and the like, with players and dealers and operators busy at them. The floor was worn and dirty, and the air was filled with smoke. Large armed guards stood at regular intervals, looking, she thought, for somebody to shoot.

"We'd better get checked in," Lando said. "Then we can come down and see just how honest this casino operation is."

"Ah, Prince Xizor," the Emperor said. "How good to see you again."

Xizor nodded and bowed low. "The pleasure is mine, my Emperor."

45

"What brings you to my chambers?"

"I was just curious, my master, as to the progress of Lord Vader's attack upon the Rebel shipyard in the Baji Sector."

The Emperor's ravaged face revealed nothing, but Xizor was certain his comment had come as a surprise.

"I really must see about hiring your spies away from you," the Emperor said.

"It was not my spies who gave me this information," Xizor replied.

"Tell me, then, how did you come to know of it?" the Emperor asked.

"I'm surprised Lord Vader didn't mention it to you. What my spies did discover was the location of the Rebel shipyard. I, of course, immediately offered this information to Lord Vader."

"Of course," the Emperor said smoothly. "I am expecting a report from the fleet shortly. Perhaps you would join in some refreshments and wait with me?"

"I would be honored."

Xizor kept his smile in check. Vader had not told the Emperor who had given him the Rebel shipyard. And he had somehow erased the recordings from the Emperor's own skyhook to keep him from finding out. Xizor himself would have done the same in Vader's position. Which was, of course, why he was here. To make certain the Emperor knew whom to credit for this bit of business.

He was going to enjoy watching Vader become aware that his little game had gone awry.

He was going to enjoy it greatly.

Vader stepped onto the holocam field and initiated a transmission. The air shimmered as the Emperor appeared.

Vader lowered himself to one knee. "My master," he said.

"Ah, Lord Vader. Your report?" the Emperor asked.

"The Rebel shipyard is no more. They put up a fight, but it was brief. We destroyed hundreds of vessels and thousands of the enemy within them."

"Good, good." The Emperor waved his hand, and his image became smaller as the holocam on his end adjusted to a wider angle. The new angle revealed Xizor standing a couple of meters away.

"Prince Xizor was just telling me how happy he was to provide the Empire with the location of the Rebel base. It seems we owe him much gratitude, don't you think?" the Emperor asked, his words rich with dark amusement.

Vader gritted his teeth and looked at Xizor. It was good that they could not see his face when he spoke. "The Empire owes you thanks, Prince Xizor."

The Emperor smiled.

Xizor smiled even more widely. "Oh, think nothing of it, Lord Vader. I am always happy to serve."

It was good that he was light-years away. Vader's anger was such that he wasn't sure he could have stopped himself from destroying Xizor had he been within reach.

"I expect to see you soon, Lord Vader," the Emperor said.

"Yes, my master. We are returning even as we speak."

"Good."

The image swirled and faded.

Vader stood and turned to leave the holo chamber.

A junior officer approached him as he exited. "Lord Vader, I—"

That was as far as he got. Vader clenched his fist and called upon the dark side.

The officer fell, clutching his throat.

"I do not wish to be disturbed," Vader said to the man lying on the deck. "Is that clear?"

Vader opened his fist.

The officer inhaled noisily. When he could manage it, he said, "C-C-Clear, L-Lord Vader!"

With that, Darth Vader stormed away to his own chamber to brood.

7

Luke was practicing with his new lightsaber when he heard a distant buzz. It was faint, but growing louder. He turned and looked into the morning desert. He could see a dust trail, leading right toward him. The buzz sounded like engines. A lot of them.

Luke circled to a sand dune and crouched down. From there he would be able to see his visitors before they saw him. Already he could tell that it was a gang of swoop riders coming to call. Swoops were narrow speeders that could hold two riders, not much more than big engines with seats and controls. They were fast and maneuverable, and outlaws often used them for escaping crime scenes, as well as for smuggling or bootlegging.

What was a gang of swoop riders doing out here? He was the only person around for a hundred kilometers. It wasn't likely they'd gotten lost. No, they were definitely coming to see him, and he didn't think it was intended to be a very neighborly visit.

The swoops roared in, and Luke saw that all the riders carried blasters. One of them spotted him, jerked his blaster up, and fired. The beam sizzled past him, not even close.

"Blow the little runt to Bespin, boys!" one of the riders yelled.

Two of the riders headed for him, both firing. Their beams missed Luke by a meter. The swoops kicked up a lot of grit. A cloud of dust surrounded them. Luke jumped and swung his glowing green blade.

A roar to his left. Luke twisted in the air. A swoop roared by, its rider holding in his hand what looked like a giant ax. Another engine screamed toward him. As the second swooper came in, Luke swung his lightsaber, faking out the rider, then slammed his boot into the man.

Luke's kick toppled the attacker from the swoop, and Luke hopped on, opened the throttle, and headed for Beggar's Canyon. He'd explored every centimeter of the place as a kid; no way they'd run him down there. He could pick them off one at a time, disable their machines— shoot, he could capture the whole gang!

The pack of swoops was still behind him when he dropped into Beggar's Canyon. The canyon was straight for nearly two kilometers before it made a sharp turn to the right. Dead Man's Turn, they called it, and for good reason. Try to take it too fast and you'd turn yourself into gooey paste on the canyon wall.

Luke took it easy as a sneeze.

At least half of the swoop gang didn't make it. But they still outnumbered him at least six to one. As he throttled back for a sharp turn, Luke heard a hoarse yell: "He's got help! We ain't gonna win this one, Spiker! Let's burn!"

Luke looked over his shoulder. A swoop, engines off,

dropped silently in free fall. The man on the machine wore black, his head shrouded in a flight helmet, a blinking blaster held in his outstretched hand as he shot at the swoopers.

The falling swoop's engines ignited. It continued to fall, but more slowly. The rider kept firing as he fell, sending the swoopers scurrying for cover. The swoop got within a few centimeters of the ground and stopped. It hovered, dead still.

Man, Luke thought, *this guy can fly.*

The swoopers took off. After a moment the stranger eased his craft toward Luke. He took off his helmet.

It was Dash Rendar.

"What are you doing here?" Luke asked.

Dash shrugged. "Saving your butt from swoop scum, it looks like," he said.

"You know what I mean," Luke said. "Why are you here?"

"Well," Dash said with a grin, "Leia wanted me to keep an eye on you until she gets back."

"She what?" Luke snapped. "Look pal, I don't need a baby-sitter."

"Oh, yeah, you coulda taken those guys by yourself, huh?" Dash teased.

"I wasn't doing so bad," Luke said.

"No, you weren't," Dash agreed, "but you were gonna lose."

Luke held his temper as best he could. He didn't like this braggart, but Dash was right. Like it or not—and he didn't like it at all—Dash had saved his neck.

"Thanks," Luke mumbled.

"Excuse me, I didn't hear what you said."

"Don't push it, Dash," Luke said.

The older man grinned.

"I was in Mos Eisley hanging around when I heard them talking," Dash said. "They had orders to kill you. I guess Vader is no longer your number one admirer."

"He never was," Luke said. "If it was him behind it."

Was it, though? Luke shook his head. That still didn't make sense.

Xizor leaned back in his chair and looked at the small holographic image floating on his desk.

Standing on his desk was a strikingly beautiful woman, unaware that her picture had been captured by a hidden holocam. Princess Leia Organa. He knew who she was, of course, though he had never bothered to scan her image before.

Behind him Guri said, "She approached the owner of one of our protected casinos on Rodia, in the gaming complex. She wants to set up a meeting with somebody of stature in Black Sun."

The Dark Prince steepled his fingers and regarded the image.

"Now, why would one of the leaders of the Alliance be interested in our organization?" he wondered aloud. "They have made it a point not to do business with us. They've never wanted to dirty their clean revolutionary hands with common criminals."

Xizor paused, then continued. "It must be important. Princess Organa is close to only a few people. One of them is Luke Skywalker. It is a strong possibility that she knows where he is. And if not, she may certainly be a useful tool in my search for him. Bring her to me."

8

"So, where is Leia?" Luke asked after he and Dash had returned to Ben's, each on a swoop.

"Gone to Rodia to connect up with Black Sun."

Luke nearly dropped the container of cold water he held. "Black Sun! Is she out of her mind? Han told me once that they were more dangerous than the Empire. Why would Leia want to contact Black Sun?"

"Got me," Dash said, and shrugged. "Maybe they know who wants you dead."

The idea of Leia fooling around with a vicious underground criminal organization bothered Luke. Still, what was he going to do about it?

"So, what's the drill, kid?" Dash asked.

"Huh?"

"We gonna sit around here and wait for them to come back? Or you maybe want to go ask the Hutt why he sent that bunch of jokers out to zap you?" Dash said, his sarcasm as biting as ever.

"Jabba's got no reason to be after me," Luke said.

"Unless somebody put him up to it. That's why I'm here," Dash reminded him. "Somebody wants you smoked."

Suddenly Artoo began whistling and beeping frantically.

"I don't like the sound of that," Luke said.

"What is it?" Dash asked.

"Something outside, sounds like. We'd better go see."

Artoo beeped again. Dash pulled his blaster. Luke reached down to touch his lightsaber, to assure himself that it was still hanging from his belt. They all moved to the door.

Outside, they saw the fire of a breaking rocket high overhead.

"Looks like a message droid," Luke said.

Message droids weren't something you had drop in on you every day. They were used when fast delivery was needed and you didn't want to risk using the HoloNet. They were expensive and good for only one shot.

The message carrier hit hard enough to splash sand and make a noise they could hear five hundred meters away. Luke and Dash started toward the ship.

The message droid, a small, compact, rounded box, hovered a couple of meters off the ground.

"I am empowered to deliver a message to Princess Leia Organa, or, in her absence, an authorized representative," it said.

"Tell me. I'm her authorized representative," Luke said.

"Password?" the droid asked.

"Uh, Luke Skywalker."

"That password is incorrect."

Dash laughed.

"Han Solo?"

"That password is incorrect."

Luke thought about it. It had to be something simple, he figured, something Leia wouldn't forget. What was the first thing that came to mind when he thought about her?

"Alderaan?"

"Password correct."

A sliding plate on the droid moved and exposed a holoprojector. After a second a hologram blinked on, showing a short, long-haired, bearded Bothan.

"Greetings, Princess Leia," the hologram said. "Koth Melan here, speaking to you from my homeworld of Bothawui. Our spy network has uncovered information vital to the Alliance. You must come to Bothawui immediately. Time is of the essence. I will be at the Intergalactic Trade Mission for five days. The Alliance must act in that time or the information may be lost."

The projection shut down.

"We need to get this information to Leia," Luke said.

"Not a chance, kid," Dash reasoned. "We can't use the HoloNet because it isn't secure and we don't know exactly where she is. And by the time we got to Rodia, found her, and got her back to Bothawui, it'd be a week at least."

"Okay, I get the picture," Luke said. "I guess we'll have to go in her place, then."

"Why? The message was for her," Dash said.

"I'm her designated representative. Whatever Koth Melan has got, he can tell it to me."

"Doesn't sound too bright to me," Dash complained.

"And his name doesn't sound right, either. Melan? That's not Bothan."

"Nobody asked you," Luke said. "You're supposed to be a bodyguard, right? You don't care about the Alliance."

"Not unless they want to hire me, you got that right," Dash agreed.

"Fine," Luke said. "I'm going. You do whatever you want."

"Well," Dash said slowly as a grin spread over his face. "You're worth more to me alive than dead; I'd better protect my fee. I'll meet you in orbit."

Luke nodded. He didn't much like Dash, but the guy was good with a gun, and he could fly. That counted for a lot.

"Let's go get the X-wing, Artoo," he said to the little droid. "We're going for a ride."

Artoo beeped and whistled. He obviously didn't think it was a particularly good idea, either.

Too bad, Luke thought. *A Jedi Knight wouldn't just sit around when there was vital Alliance business in the works, would he?*

No. He wouldn't.

Luke had never been on Bothawui, and he was surprised at how clean and well maintained it was compared to his homeworld. It was a sunny spring day locally. There was a token force of Imperial stormtroopers hanging around in small groups, but it seemed as if the Bothans had control of the port itself. The streets were wide, and many of the tall buildings were glittery with some kind of natural stone.

After asking around a bit, he and Dash found their way to Koth Melan's office, where a protocol droid much like Threepio greeted them pleasantly.

"Good morning," the droid said. "How may I assist you?"

"Princess Leia is supposed to see Koth Melan," Luke said.

"You are Princess Leia?"

Luke frowned. "No, no, I'm not Princess Leia. I'm her . . . representative. Luke Skywalker. Koth Melan wants to see her, so he'll want to see us."

The droid said, "I don't believe that is a logical assumption."

"Look, just tell him we're here, okay?"

"I'm afraid I cannot admit you without an appointment," the droid said stiffly. "Master Melan is a very busy Bothan. Perhaps I can arrange for you to see him in, oh, perhaps a week? Your names?"

Luke frowned again. How could they convince this droid to let them in? Couldn't bribe him, the Force wouldn't work . . .

Dash grinned and pulled his blaster. He pointed it at the droid. "Okay, Goldie. My name is Man with a Blaster About to Cook You. Either you open the door or your busy Bothan is going to have to get himself a new receptionist."

"Oh, dear," the droid said.

"And no security alarms, either," Dash said. "I'm watching you real carefully. Hurry up, and do the door manually."

The protocol droid said, "Very well, Man with a Blaster About to Cook You."

Luke and Dash exchanged amused looks. Droids could be too literal at times.

The droid tapped a code into the keypad next to the inner door. It slid open.

"Inside," Dash ordered.

They followed the droid into a large office. Sitting behind a desk was the Bothan who'd sent the message to Leia.

"Master Melan, I'm sorry to interrupt, but—"

"It's all right, R0-4. Go back to your desk. I'll see these gentlemen."

The droid left, closing the door behind him.

"Excuse the way we came in," Luke said, stepping forward, "but we had to see you."

Melan smiled. "I know. You're Luke Skywalker, and you're Dash Rendar. I've been expecting you. I know your reputation and your work for the Alliance. Please, take a seat."

Luke and Dash exchanged quick glances.

"Perhaps I should explain," Melan continued. "I discovered that Princess Organa was no longer on Tatooine a short time ago, too late to recall the messenger droid I sent. Because you are here, I assume you knew the password she and I agreed upon. You're here, and now we can get to the business at hand."

Luke moved to one of the chairs and sat. Dash did the same.

"The Empire has embarked on a new military project," Melan began. "We do not yet know what or where the project is, but we do know it is vast. The Emperor has diverted huge amounts of money, material, and men for this secret enterprise."

"How did you come by this information?" Luke asked.

"The Bothan spynet is second to none," Melan said. There seemed to be a touch of pride in his voice. "The plans are kept closely guarded in special computers with no outside lines. From what little else we've learned of it, this project does not bode well for the Alliance."

Luke nodded. "So, what are we supposed to do about it?"

"Our operatives have discovered that one of the secured computers is being sent from Imperial Center to Bothawui. We believe the Alliance would be served by obtaining this computer and cracking it open, to see what the Empire is up to."

Luke nodded again. "That sounds reasonable."

"Excuse me," Dash said. "But why are you so hot to help out the Alliance? I thought the Bothan spynet's job was to gather and sell information, not get involved with strategy and tactics."

Melan looked grim. "Twenty years ago, the Empire had my father executed for espionage," he said.

"That's one of the risks of this business, isn't it?" Dash asked.

"Yes, and one I take," Melan answered. "But not all Bothans are spies, Rendar. My father was nothing more than a teacher. Until the Empire is defeated, I can have no true honor. And I would think," he continued, "that you might have a grudge against the Empire yourself. After what the Emperor did to you and your family."

Dash gritted his teeth; Luke saw his jaw muscles flex. "That's none of your business," he said.

Luke said nothing, but the question leaped to his mind: *What* did *they do to you, Dash?*

Instead, he said, "If the Empire is going to all this trouble, we'd better find out why. How do we get our hands on this computer?"

Melan nodded. "The Empire is transporting the computer on an unescorted ship disguised as a simple freighter carrying fertilizer. Such a ship will not draw the attention of the Alliance the way a heavily armed convoy would. Our operatives inform us that they will be able to obtain the route of the disguised ship shortly. When they do, it will only be a day or two before the vessel arrives. It would help if we had a commander with some experience in space battles to lead us."

Luke smiled. "That's me." He turned to Dash. "What about you? You in? One freighter against a squad of Bothans and me in my X-wing. How dangerous can it be?"

Dash appeared to consider it.

"Besides," Luke continued, "if the information in the computer is as valuable as it seems to be, the Alliance might be willing to give you a bonus for helping collect it. Could be worth a few thousand credits, maybe more."

"All right," Dash said with a shrug. "I got nothing else to do. Why not?"

Luke grinned. This guy did remind him an awful lot of Han Solo.

9

Leia was so bored, she was contemplating putting a credit coin into one of the rigged gambling machines.

Avaro approached her. "I just got a comm fwom off-planet. Black Thune'th wepwethentative ith en woute. Thee will be hewah in thwee dayth."

Leia felt a rush of relief. Thank goodness. Then, as Avaro waddled off, she thought about what he'd just said.

"Thee" will be here in three days?

She?

Well, why not? No rule said a woman couldn't be a criminal.

Luke led the Bothan squad away from the planet in the sensor shadow of the local moon, to help them avoid Imperial patrols. He turned his attention to the ambush.

Behind him Dash flew his chrome ship, with Koth Melan as a passenger.

"Keep in tight, boys," Luke said into his comm. "We're almost on station. Let's hear you sound off, Blue Squad."

The pilots logged in. He'd kept it simple: Each of the attack ships got a number, and he'd christened the unit with a color.

"Copy," Luke said. "We're there. Stall 'em in position."

Blue Squad obeyed, bringing their fighters to a halt. They floated in the middle of nowhere, waiting. If their information was correct, the freighter ought to be popping out of hyperspace less than a hundred kilometers dead ahead . . .

The freighter pilot must have overslept. The ship dropped into realspace, all right, but only fifty klicks away.

"Heads up, Blue Squad, there's our target. Attack formation!"

The ship came out of hyperspace relatively slowly, but since it was closer than anticipated, they didn't have much time. Luke switched to a standard operations channel and hailed the freighter.

"Attention onboard the freighter *Suprosa*. This is Commander Skywalker of the Alliance. Shut down your engines and prepare to be boarded."

"This is the captain of the freighter *Suprosa*. Are you crazy?" came the reply. "We're hauling fertilizer here! What kind of pirates are you?"

"We're not pirates. Like I said, we are with the Alliance. And maybe we have a big garden. Pull it up, Captain, and nobody gets hurt."

There came a long pause. It was possible the pilot didn't know what he was hauling, but Luke didn't believe that.

"Listen, pal, I'm working under contract to XTS, and my orders are to deliver my cargo to the agent on Bothawui. Why don't you go bother somebody smuggling guns or something?" the freighter captain said.

"Captain, either you shut down your engines or we'll shut them down for you. Some of my gunners can pick flies off a wall with their laser cannons." Well, it was possible, though he hadn't seen any of them shooting quite that well during maneuvers. But the freighter pilot didn't know that.

The freighter suddenly dropped its cargo module, speeded up, and turned to starboard.

It was going to make a run for it.

Luke switched back to the tactical channel. "Gotta do it the hard way, boys. Target the engines only! If you aren't sure, don't take the shot—we don't want to blow this baby up. Move in!"

The distance between Blue Squadron and the freighter decreased in a hurry. This was stupid. The ship was unarmed and much slower than the Alliance ships. If they wanted to cook the captain, he was dinner—and he had to know it.

Artoo whistled.

"Put it onscreen, Artoo." The image of the freighter appeared on Luke's screen. Where there had been four smooth sections of hull, red lights now blinked. Two other spots flashed blue. Plates had slid back on the freighter to reveal hidden weapons.

"Heads up, everybody, this thing has got teeth! He's got laser cannons fore and aft and what looks like missile launchers ventral and dorsal. Watch yourselves!"

Luke put his X-wing into a sweeping turn as the freighter's port laser fired. The blast was close enough to scramble his comm.

The freighter was not such an easy target after all.

"Break off, circle, and regroup!" Luke called into his comm.

Blue Two was on the way in, and it halted its attack run.

Too late. Blue Two and Blue Four became shattered history. Four of the Bothan ships looped away in pretty good formation, the *Outrider* along with them. Luke was close enough to see the missile port on top of the freighter blow a cloud of gas into space that crystallized and glittered under the local sun's light.

"He's got a missile off!" Luke yelled.

"I got it!" Dash said.

Luke watched Dash's ship roll and dive, and his robotic guns began spewing bolts of energy. He couldn't see the missile, but he saw Dash continuing his attack, saw the guns spraying their energy spears.

"Blast!" Dash cursed. "I've got to be hitting it! Why doesn't it stop?"

"Dash! Come on!" Luke yelled.

"Shut up, I've got it! Stop, you blasted piece of junk. Stop!"

"Incoming!" Blue Six yelled. "Scatter!"

The four fighters tried to split up, separating like an opening fist.

Too late. The missile exploded among them, and when the blast cleared, all four ships and eight Bothans were gone.

"I can't have missed," Dash said, his voice filled with disbelief. "I can't."

Anger swept over Luke as he put the X-wing into a sharp and twisting turn. He headed right at the freighter. Six of his squadron had been destroyed, just like that. And Dash, hotshot Dash, he'd messed up royally.

Luke was too angry to use the Force. He ignored the energy beams stabbing at him, ignored Artoo's whistles and bleats, ignored everything but the engine compartment of the freighter under his guns. He fired and fired again. He saw the radiation absorbed by the shields and the blue glow brighten. The force field gave way under his attack. The engine compartment ruptured, smoked, and flashed red and purple as his laser beams baked and killed it.

"I couldn't have missed," Dash said. He sounded dazed.

"Stow it, Dash," Luke ordered. "It's too late to worry about it now."

Luke switched channels. To the freighter he said, "Your engines are dead, Captain, and that's what you and your crew will be if you fire another laser or missile, do you copy?"

A brief pause. "We copy."

"You are hereby considered prisoners of war. Stand by to be boarded. If you value your lives, don't mess with your real cargo."

Luke shut off his comm. *Oh, man.* He'd lost half his squad. He should have known it was too easy to be true. A dozen Bothans had died to secure this vessel and its computer. He should have been ready for a trick. He should have known better than to trust the Empire. He should have realized that Dash was more talk than substance.

He shook his head. He hoped whatever was in the computer it was carrying was worth what it had cost to collect it. It had better be.

Leia approached Chewie where he was playing a board game with Threepio, the other gamblers in the place having been convinced it was wiser to let the Wookiee win than not.

"Let's go, boys. We have company."

Chewie and Threepio stood and followed her from the casino.

Lando was on the way to their rented suite, to do another fast pass on the place and to set up security. He'd be hiding with his blaster drawn when the Black Sun rep showed up. Chewie would watch the door from the hall, and Threepio would stay with Leia. Lando, blaster in hand, met them at the door when they buzzed.

"Everything set?" she asked.

"Yes," he said. He waved at the suite's meeting room. There was a desk with a computer inset at one end of the room, two couches, three chairs, and a small table. A bar and a cooler were tucked into the corner opposite the door. Two sliding doors led to the refresher and an adjoining bedroom. "I'll be behind the bedroom door," Lando said. "In case the Black Sun rep needs to use the refresher."

Leia moved to the desk and sat behind it. Might as well

try to keep this on a businesslike basis. She sat, took a deep breath, blew it out.

Chewie called from the hallway. Their caller had arrived.

"Send her in," Leia said.

The computer was the size of a small carrying case. It was black and nearly featureless, except for a control panel along one edge. Koth Melan held the thing easily on his palms.

They were on board the *Outrider* in the ship's lounge. Dash sprawled in a chair, staring at the wall, not saying anything. He was stunned at his failure to stop the missile that had taken out four Bothan ships.

Luke also stared, but at the small computer. Once again, he hoped whatever was in it was worth the lives of a dozen Bothans.

"Can you access the program?" Luke asked.

Melan shook his head. "No. It will be encrypted and protected by an automatic destruct device. Only an expert can get to it. Our best computer team is on Kothlis, a Bothan colony world a few light-years from here. We'll transport it there and find out what we've got."

"I'd like to go along," Luke said.

"Of course. I'll give you coordinates; you can reach it easily in your X-wing."

"Dash?" Luke said.

The man didn't answer but continued to stare at nothing. This had really hit him hard. Luke actually felt sorry for him.

"Dash," he said again.

"Huh?" Dash said, and blinked, as if coming out of a trance.

Luke had seen it before. Battle shock.

To Melan Luke said, "Would it be possible for your organization to locate Princess Leia?"

"As of yesterday, she was at Avaro Sookcool's casino in the gambling complex on Rodia."

Luke shook his head. These guys were good. He looked at Dash. He couldn't bring him along, not the way he was now. Dash was in no condition for another firefight.

"Dash . . ."

"I had it in my sights," Dash said. "No way I could have missed."

"Dash!"

"Huh? What?"

"Go to Rodia. Find Princess Leia and tell her about the computer and the secret plans," Luke instructed. "You got it?"

"I should go with you," Dash protested weakly.

"No," Luke said, feeling as if he were talking to a child. "It's more important that you find the princess."

Dash stared at Luke. "All right. Rodia. Plans. Got it."

"We'll meet later," Luke said. "Okay?"

"Meet you later," Dash mumbled. "Uh-huh."

"You going to be all right?" Luke asked.

"Yeah."

Luke turned back to Melan, who appeared sympathetic.

"It is war," the Bothan said. "Bad things happen."

Luke nodded. Just one more thing the Empire had to answer for.

Whatever she had been expecting, Leia thought, Guri was not it. The woman from Black Sun was beautiful, with long blond hair and a trim figure. She wore a short black cloak and boots, with a red leather belt slung low over her hips. If she had a weapon, Leia couldn't spot it.

Guri sat across from Leia and smiled. Her voice was cool and even. "How may we serve you, Princess?"

"I understand that Black Sun has a first-rate intelligence-gathering capability," Leia said.

Guri flashed a smile. "We hear things from time to time."

"Care for some refreshment?" Leia nodded toward the bar and Threepio.

"Tea if it's not too much trouble. Hot."

Leia looked at Threepio. "And the same for me, please."

"At once," Threepio said, and began making the tea.

"Your flight was pleasant?" Leia asked.

Guri smiled. "Very. I trust Avaro has made your wait here equally pleasant?"

The tea came and went, the conversation stayed bland, and although Leia couldn't quite put her finger on it, something was wrong. Guri didn't feel right, somehow. She was polite and agreeable enough, but Leia still couldn't wait to be rid of her visitor. So far they hadn't come near the subject of Luke and who wanted him dead. Eventually she'd have to work her way to that, but not yet. Not until she could get a handle on what was bothering her about Guri.

Guri leaned forward. "I regret that I must ask if it might be possible to continue this meeting later. I have pressing business on one of the local moons, and I'm afraid my launch window is coming up soon."

"Of course," Leia said.

"Perhaps we can talk again in, say, three or four days?" Guri suggested.

"I will look forward to it," Leia said, smiling.

After Guri was gone, Lando and Chewie came into the room.

"What do you think?" Leia said.

"Man, she's a smooth piece of work," Lando replied. "You could stack ice cubes on her head and they wouldn't melt. She's very attractive, but there's something spooky about her."

Leia nodded. She was glad Lando had noticed.

"Threepio?"

"I was unable to place her accent," he said. "Which is decidedly odd, given my extensive experience in languages. Her speech was flawless, her inflection precise, but I am afraid I cannot tell you her planet of origin."

Chewie said something. It was clear he didn't like her, either. And few things made a Wookiee nervous.

Maybe the next time the woman from Black Sun visited, they ought to prepare their reception a little better.

Luke's X-wing dropped from hyperspace in the vicinity of the planet Kothlis. It did not appear to be swarming with Imperial Navy, at least not where Luke was. He scanned the local comm bands and picked up normal traffic, nothing alarming.

"Artoo, lay in a course for the rendezvous Melan gave us."

Artoo whistled his acknowledgment.

"You sure this thing is going to work?" Leia asked.

Chewbacca, busy working on the doorjamb with a small power wrench, said something. It sounded snide.

Threepio quickly translated: "He says that if it doesn't, it won't be because it was improperly installed."

Leia turned and looked at Lando, who shrugged.

"The guy who sold it to me said it was top-of-the-line," he said. "Got the latest magno scanner, full-range sensor, a self-contained power supply good for a year. It better work, it cost me enough."

Chewie gargled something.

"He says it is ready for testing," Threepio said.

Leia walked to the desk and sat behind it. The

computer inset into the desk was off, and she switched it on.

"The unit is under the file 'Bioscan,' " Lando said.

Leia looked down at the desk. The words *Scanner offline* appeared on the screen. It would be invisible from the chair opposite the desk. "Bioscan on," she said.

"Okay, everybody out. Let's test it."

Threepio, Lando, and Chewie trooped out into the hall.

"Okay," Leia yelled. "Lando, you come in first."

The door opened, and Lando sauntered in. He turned around as if modeling the latest fashions. "Here I am. Enjoy."

Leia grinned. He was endearing for a scoundrel. She looked down at the screen.

The scanner newly inset into the frame of the door picked up Lando's image, and it appeared on the screen. An infocrawl moved up the side of the image as the sensors examined Lando and fed the result to the computer: Human, male, armed with a blaster and a small vibro-shiv in his pants pocket on the left side, heartbeat, respiration, muscle tone index, height, weight, body temperature. Even a refractive index indicating how old his skin was, plus or minus a year.

Lando, according to this device, was a little older than he looked. There were no bombs or poison gas hidden upon his person. No hidden holocams or recording devices.

"Seems to be working on you. Chewie, come on in."

Again the device scanned and reported. She didn't

know what the normal readings for a Wookiee were, but the program that came with the scanner apparently did, and it told her that Chewie was within normal limits for one of that species.

Finally she called Threepio in. The program had no trouble at all recognizing him as a droid.

"Well. It seems to be working just fine," she said.

Lando's comlink beeped. He pulled it from his belt, lifted the comlink, and said, "Go ahead."

"A ship has just arrived," a shrill voice said. "The *Outrider*."

"Dash Rendar?" Leia said. "What is he doing here? He's supposed to be watching Luke."

They met Dash halfway.

"Is Luke okay?" Leia asked in a rush.

"Yeah, he's fine," Dash replied.

"Why are you here? You're supposed to be guarding him," she said.

"He's fine," Dash said, staring at her. "He doesn't need *my* help."

"You don't look so good," Lando remarked. "Trouble?"

Dash explained. When he was finished, Leia shook her head. Luke was okay, that was the important thing.

Well. As soon as this business with Black Sun was finished, they would go and find Luke. Somehow it would all get sorted out.

———

"Hey, hey, hey!" one of the Bothan techs said. "Look at this, boys! Scan sector T-H-X."

Luke heard the tap of keys, shouted commands. It looked as if the Bothans were about to find out exactly what was in the computer data that they had gone to so much trouble to hijack.

"Wow!" said one of the other techs.

"Oh, sister," said another. "I can't believe it!"

"What?" Luke said. "What is it?"

Before anybody could say, the door exploded inward and somebody came in shooting.

Leia smiled at Guri, who was seated across from her at the desk in their suite. But the smile was to cover her puzzlement. According to the computer screen inset into the desk and the scanner that fed it, Guri was not human. What she was, the scanner program could not say.

"Care for some refreshment?" Leia asked.

"Tea would be fine."

"Threepio, fix two cups of the special tea blend, would you, please?"

Leia turned back from the droid and flashed her smile at Guri again. She caught the computer screen peripherally as she glanced at Black Sun's representative. According to the scanner, Guri's skin was only ten years old.

It would be no trouble to keep Guri talking for a few minutes, until the "special blend" tea Threepio was preparing did its job. The sleeping potion he was putting in Guri's cup would put her out harmlessly for a couple of hours, during which time Leia and the others could make a closer examination of Guri's person and effects. At least Leia's instincts had been right: There was something odd about Guri. Very odd.

Threepio brought the tea. Leia hoped the droid had gotten the stuff into the right cup. It would be embarrassing if Lando or Chewie needed to come in and take over while she took a nap.

After twenty minutes of small talk, Leia realized the sleeping potion wasn't going to work. It was supposed to take five minutes—eight minutes at the outside, if you had the constitution of a rock. Guri continued their diplomatic back-and-forth without any apparent effects from the potion.

The computer was still processing information and displaying it for Leia. The being sitting across from her breathed air, and her heart pumped blood, but the lungs weren't normal, and neither was the heart. The muscles under the supposedly-ten-year-old skin weren't made of any tissue the scanner could recognize.

No doubt about it, this was a problem, and not one that Leia had anticipated.

Guri helped her resolve the problem. She said, "All right, Leia Organa, I think this has gone on long enough."

"Excuse me?"

Guri held up her empty container. As Leia watched, she squeezed the heavy ceramic mug in one hand. Her hand shook a little, but the cup shattered into tiny bits. Guri smiled. "I can do that to your head if I wish. You probably have a weapon hidden somewhere, but I warn you, I am much faster than you. I can get to you before you get to it."

Leia played it out. "Suppose I believe you. What do you want?"

"You are going to accompany me from this place. You will tell the Wookiee in the hall to stay here as we leave. Convince him; otherwise he dies," Guri said with a cold smile.

"Where are we going?"

"Do not concern yourself with that. Just do as you are told," Guri said.

"I don't think so," Leia said. "Lando? Dash?"

The door to the bedroom slid open. Lando and Dash stood there, blasters aimed at Guri. They stepped into the room. The door to the hall also slid open, and Chewie stood there with his bowcaster leveled at Guri's back.

"You'd have to be real fast to avoid being hit by three bolts," Leia said.

Guri turned her head slightly to glance at Chewie, then turned back to look at Leia. "You have the advantage, it would seem. What do you propose?"

It was a good question. What were they going to do now?

One of the Bothan techs leaped up, grabbed the computer, and jerked it loose from the leads. The screens went blank.

"Go!" Melan yelled at the tech. "We'll cover you!"

The tech ran for the rear of the room. A section of the

wall slid back to reveal an unmarked emergency exit. The tech with the computer barreled through the opening.

Melan, meanwhile, emptied the charge in his blaster at the attackers who were still pouring in. The weapon clicked dry, and he tossed it aside.

Luke ignited his lightsaber and chopped the blaster from the hand of the first man to reach them. He wondered briefly why the man didn't cook them, but had no time to reflect on it as five or six more shooters came in.

There were ten, fifteen of them now, all pointing blasters at him but not firing. What—?

"Turn off your saber," one of them commanded in a rough voice. "You can't win."

Luke saw that he didn't have a chance, even using the Force. He clicked off his lightsaber. One of them moved in and removed the lightsaber from his grasp.

Luke looked back at the man. "What do you want?"

"Sorry, but we want you, Skywalker."

"You're going to dance into the heart of the Empire, just like that?" Dash asked.

"I have some connections at Imperial Center," Leia said. "That's where our friend here came from." She nodded at Guri, who offered nothing.

"Somebody is playing games I don't much like. Luke is in danger; this . . . person who says she represents Black Sun is our only link to them."

"How are you going to get there?" Dash asked. "Book a compartment on a liner? They check those things going into Imperial Center, you know."

"Excuse me," Guri said. "There is an easier way."

Leia stared at her, then at the others. "What are you talking about?"

"You want to go to Imperial Center and meet with the leadership of Black Sun, correct?" Guri asked.

"That was the general idea," Leia answered.

"That is why I was sent—to provide you escort for such a trip."

"Then why the threats?" Leia asked, uncertain.

"It was the fastest way," Guri answered.

"I wouldn't trust her, Leia," Lando said.

"I don't, but I'm reasonable. Go on."

"It will be very risky for you to try to sneak into Imperial Center. I can greatly lessen that risk."

"No offense, but Lando is right. Why should we trust you?"

"Because I work for Prince Xizor," Guri said.

Lando and Dash both inhaled sharply. Leia looked at them.

"Xizor is the *head* of Black Sun," Dash said.

"You are wanted by the Empire, as are your companions. I can arrange disguises, get you past customs and straight to the prince," Guri said. "It would eliminate much of the risk."

"Why does Xizor want to see me?" Leia asked.

"You have been showing interest in Black Sun, and Prince Xizor has an interest in the Alliance. As a token of his goodwill, he wishes to offer you information about the attempted assassination of Luke Skywalker. A friend of yours, is he not?"

Xizor knew about the plot! "We are comrades, yes," Leia said. "How do you know about the attempts on Luke Skywalker's life?"

"I do not. Prince Xizor has knowledge of this, and offers it to you, but he insists that you discuss it face to face," Guri explained.

Leia looked around the room. This certainly was unexpected. What was she going to do?

11

Luke was locked in a cell. A guard nearly two meters tall and probably a meter wide stood across the hall with a blast rifle, staring at the door's barred window. There was a heavy plastic cot bolted to the floor, with a thin pad and a blanket on it. A dim light overhead cast faint and fuzzy shadows.

Suddenly the lock on the cell door clicked and the door swung inward. The reptilian Barabel who had been in command stepped into view.

"I don't suppose you want to tell me what's going on?" Luke asked.

"No reason why not," the Barabel answered. "There's nothing you can do about it. I am Skahtul. I make my living as a bounty hunter. It seems there is a large reward—a very large reward—offered to whoever delivers Luke Skywalker to them, alive and well, no questions asked."

Before Luke could speak, she continued: "Oddly enough, there is a second reward being offered for Luke Skywalker—this one is for you dead. Fortunately for you, the second amount is not quite as large as the first, so we plan to keep you healthy until we can collect it."

With that, the Barabel oozed back through the door and locked it tight.

Luke stared after her. Well, this was great. Captured by a bunch of bounty hunters and sold to the highest bidder. Good thing the one who wanted him dead—and who might that be?—was not as generous as whoever wanted him alive. Since a lot of money was involved, he had an idea about who the latter could be.

Darth Vader could throw credits out a window and never miss them. Luke had better think of something fast. He had an idea that if he stood face to face with Vader unarmed, he wasn't going to have much of a chance of surviving the meeting.

The Emperor sat in his favorite throne, the one set a meter higher than the rest of the room. Vader entered and dropped to one knee.

"My master."

"Rise, Lord Vader."

Vader did so. He hoped whatever the Emperor wanted was something easy and brief. He had just received word from his agents that Luke had been found. His captors, it seemed, were a ragtag band of bounty hunters who were demanding more money. Vader's agents knew who they were but not precisely where they were hiding. And it seemed there was another bidder who also wanted Luke. Vader would have his people offer whatever it took. Money meant nothing when compared to the dark side. And the dark side would have Luke Skywalker, no matter the cost.

He considered going to collect Luke himself, to Kothlis, where he was reportedly being held, but to leave Imperial Center just now would be dangerous. He needed to be here to watch Xizor. The criminal's twisted plans had ensnared the Emperor, and to walk away might be a fatal mistake.

"You will go to Kothlis," the Emperor said. "And collect young Skywalker."

Vader had not expected to hear this. How did the Emperor know?

Unless . . . unless the Emperor was the other bidder for Luke?

No. That made no sense. The Emperor had given the task to Vader. He would not enter into a bidding war against himself.

Surely Prince Xizor's foul hand was involved in this. It would not be wise to bring that up; the Emperor had made it quite clear that the Dark Prince was his concern, and it would not be a good idea to reveal that Vader had plans of his own concerning Xizor.

"There is another reason for your journey. You are aware that the plans for the Death Star have fallen into Rebel hands?"

"Yes, my master."

"As it happens, our spies inform us that the plans have been transported from the freighter hijacked off Bothawui to Kothlis. Quite a coincidence, don't you think?"

That Luke and the stolen plans were on the same planet at the same time, a coincidence? Doubtful.

"We must recover those plans," the Emperor continued. "Therefore your trip will serve two purposes. Fetch Skywalker and the plans. If you cannot recover the plans, destroy Kothlis as an example to those who might sympathize with the Rebels."

Vader was displeased. "Any of our admirals could command this mission," he said. "I have many pressing matters here."

"More pressing than my commands, Lord Vader?" the Emperor asked, his eyes narrowing.

So much for that idea. "No, my master."

"I thought not. I will have Skywalker with us or destroyed, the sooner the better."

"Yes, my master."

Vader left the chamber, and his simmering anger threatened to bubble up and overcome him. Once again, Xizor had manipulated the Emperor. With Vader on Kothlis, who knew what webs that reptilian spider would spin for the Emperor?

Vader resolved to make it a fast trip.

Luke took several cleansing breaths, as he had been taught, and tried to release his thoughts at the same time. He took another breath, let half of it out, and allowed the Force to connect him to the mind of the guard in the hall.

The sensation was strange, as it always was. It was not as if he were really in two places at once, but more as if there were a part of his own mind that was somehow not quite connected.

Luke became aware that the guard's feet hurt, that he was tired of standing here holding a blast rifle watching the door when there was no way anybody could get through it, no way . . .

"Open the door," Luke said.

"Huh? Who's there?"

"You must put down your rifle and open the door now," Luke urged.

"I must . . . put down my rifle. Open the door now."

Luke watched the guard through the barred window. Watched him put his rifle down. *Got him,* Luke thought, and grinned. A mistake.

"What?" the guard said, confused.

Lost him. Concentrate, Luke!

"Open the door."

Luke put thoughts of victory and loss out of his mind. The only thing that mattered was the guard.

The guard's keycard slipped into the slot. The lock clicked.

"You're very tired. You need to come in and lie on the cot and take a nice nap," Luke told him, his voice, his very will, flowing to the guard through the Force.

"Cot. Take a nap . . ."

The guard moved into the cell and walked past Luke. Luke took the keycard from the guard's hand. He glanced out into the corridor. Nobody else around. He stepped out of the cell, shut the door carefully, dropped the keycard on the floor, and picked up the blast rifle. He looked back. The guard snored on the cot.

He ought to head straight for the nearest exit and leave. With any luck it would be hours before anybody even knew he was gone. But he wanted to see if he could find his lightsaber first. He'd spent a lot of time building it. The Force was with him. He could do it.

It was almost too easy, Luke thought, as he picked his lightsaber up from the table. The little storage room was empty, no one seemed to be awake or about, and there was his comlink right there on the table. He would call Artoo, have him warm up the X-wing and send Luke a homing signal. Once he got into his ship, these cloobs would never catch him again.

Luke put the blast rifle on the table and reached for his comlink.

"Who's there? Move and I'll shoot!"

Uh-oh.

12

Luke still held his lightsaber loosely in his right hand. He gripped the weapon more tightly, thumb on the control, as he slowly turned around to face the owner of the voice behind him.

"Sorry, I thought this was the 'fresher," Luke said.

The alien facing him was a Nikto. His horn-rimmed eyes went wide as he recognized Luke. He pulled out his blaster.

Luke thumbed the lightsaber control. The glowing blade added its light to the dim room.

The Nikto fired, and a red bolt speared at Luke. He let the Force flow, and the bolt ricocheted from his blade and hit the shooter in the foot. The Nikto dropped his weapon and began hopping on his good foot, yelling.

So much for sneaking out undetected.

Luke ran at the injured shooter, hit him with his shoulder in passing, and knocked him sprawling. Doors began to open into the hallway, and armed bounty hunters, most of them dressed for sleep, emerged.

Luke swung the lightsaber and cut a path to freedom. He ran down the hall, and the shooters ahead of him gave way against their own reflected firepower. Luke didn't know how far he had to go to get to the exit.

Ahead and to his left, the wall suddenly shattered and imploded. Smoking debris spattered in all directions. Smoke filled the corridor.

"Luke!"

He knew that voice.

"Lando? Over here!" Luke called.

Yet another blaster joined the fray, only this one wasn't aimed at Luke. Bounty hunters fell. Luke saw Lando striding through the smoke and smelly vapor.

"You called for a cab?" Lando said with a grin.

"Me? What makes you think I want to leave? I'm having fun here." Luke pivoted and chopped the barrel off an outthrust blaster. The weapon began to hiss and spew sparks, and the startled owner dropped it and fled.

Lando led the way, blaster working. Luke followed, blocking shots from behind. They went through the ruptured wall and into the night.

"I've got a, uh, borrowed landspeeder parked over there," Lando said. "The *Falcon* is in the middle of a public park five minutes away. I left Threepio watching it."

"Threepio? Where are Leia and Chewie?"

"That's a long story. Better we get back to the ship before I tell it," Lando said.

"How'd you know where to find me?" Luke asked.

"Dash gave me the planet. I got here and found out

about the raid on the Bothan safe house. I know a few locals who owed me favors. It wasn't hard from there."

Lando ducked. A blaster beam sizzled overhead and missed by a good two meters. "Can we go now?" he asked.

"Good idea."

They ran to the speeder. As they sped off, the bounty hunters kept shooting.

"It's so good to see that you are all right, Master Luke," Threepio said as they boarded the *Falcon*.

"Good to see you, too, Threepio," Luke said.

Lando hurried past them toward the *Falcon*'s cockpit. "Move it, Luke," Lando called back. "Not only do we have the bounty hunters to worry about, there's an Imperial convoy heading this way. They've just dropped out of lightspeed and into the system."

Luke ran to the control seat and sat, strapping himself down.

"Yeah? Anybody we know?" He was already reaching for preflight switches.

"I didn't get close enough to read nameplates, but the lead ship is a Star Destroyer," Lando said.

"*Victory*-class?" Luke asked.

"Bigger than that."

"*Imperial*-class?"

"Try again," Lando said.

Luke looked away from the controls at Lando, eyes going wide. "No."

"Yep. *Super*-class," Lando informed him.

"Is it . . . *Executor*?" Luke asked hesitantly.

"Like I said, I didn't get that close. But how many of those are there? They don't crank those babies up just for fun," Lando observed.

Luke stared into infinity. Was it Darth Vader? What would he be doing here?

"Let's finish the flight check fast," Lando said. "I don't think we want to stick around here."

"I hear that. Wait. I have to make a call. Artoo is in my X-wing."

"I know, I spotted it. I've got a tractor beam with his name on it. I'll overfly the X-wing and pull it up. We'll stow it in the hull clips." Lando pointed at the control screen. "We're going to slingshot out of here and hit light-speed fast. Even if it isn't Vader on that monster, we don't want to tangle with it."

Luke nodded and reached for the comm. "Where are we going?"

"Back to Tatooine. That's where Leia wants us to go."

"Where is she?"

"Let's talk about that later, okay?" Lando touched controls, listened as the ship's engines came online.

"Better sit down back there, Threepio!" Lando yelled. "We are about to be gone!"

A hundred stormtroopers surrounded the building, blasters ready to cook anybody who twitched.

Darth Vader stood in the darkness, staring at the breach that had been blown in the building's wall. He didn't need to go inside to know that Luke was not there. If the boy had been anywhere within fifty kilometers he would certainly have felt him.

Vader was not pleased.

The commander of the stormtroopers stood nervously nearby, waiting for a command.

"Bring me the highest-ranking survivor," Vader ordered.

"At once, my lord." The commander waved, and a squad moved into the building. Shots were exchanged. Time passed.

Two troopers emerged, dragging a man between them. They brought him to where Vader stood and released him. The prisoner tottered but stayed on his feet.

"Do you know who I am?" Vader asked.

"Y-Y-Yes, Lord Vader," the man stammered.

He glared at the bounty hunter. "I understand that someone else wanted Skywalker. Who?"

"I—I don't know, Lord Vader—"

Vader raised his hand and started to curl his fingers into a fist.

"Wait! Please!" the man begged. "I don't know. We—We dealt with agents."

Vader looked at the bounty hunter. Felt something more there.

"You have a suspicion," Vader said. Not a question.

"I—Some of us heard rumors. I don't know if they are true."

"Tell me."

"We heard that it was . . . Black Sun."

Vader stared at the man. *Of course.*

"And this other . . . bidder wanted Skywalker alive and well?" Vader asked.

"No, my lord. They wanted him dead."

Abruptly Vader turned away, the prisoner forgotten. Of course. It made perfect sense. Xizor wanted to thwart Vader in any manner he could. What better way than to kill his son, and by the same act, embarrass him in front of the Emperor?

"Back to the shuttle," Vader said to the commander.

"What about this scum?" The commander waved at the prisoner.

"Leave him. He is worthless."

Vader was already walking away.

Lando broke from orbit and headed out into interplanetary space.

"Did the bounty hunters get the computer?" Lando asked.

"I don't think so. I don't think they even knew it was there. Last I saw, one of the Bothan techs had the computer. I believe he escaped with it."

"If he did, the Bothans will get it to the Alliance," Lando said. "They're pretty dependable."

"I guess we'll find out what was in it eventually."

Guri led Leia and Chewie into the Imperial Center's vast Underground. Leia was disguised as an Ubese bounty hunter, complete with helmet and built-in voice scrambler. Chewie had trimmed the fur on his head into a short spacer's cut.

They walked for hours, turning and twisting into narrower and narrower corridors. Eventually they came to a heavy, locked gate, which Guri opened. She locked the gate behind them, and they moved into what looked like a small repulsor train station.

A man waited there. He was short, squat, and bald and had a blaster strapped on his left hip.

"Go with him," Guri said.

"Where are you going?" Leia asked.

"Not your business," Guri replied. "Just do as you are told and you will see Prince Xizor soon enough."

She turned and walked away without another word.

The bald man came over to stand in front of Leia. "This way," he said.

He led them to a small motorized cart parked outside. They drove into a tunnel halfway around the circle of shops. They drove for a long time.

Leia looked at Chewie and wished she could read his expressions better. He looked calm. Calmer than she felt.

They came to a stop inside a vast chamber, as big as a state ballroom. The platform at which they stopped had six large guards on it, each dressed in gray armor and carrying a blast rifle. Their driver stepped out of the cart. "This way," he said.

Two of the guards broke away from the others and moved behind Chewie and Leia.

The driver led them down a corridor that joined a maze of other hallways. Halfway through an intricate chain of left and right turns, the lights went out. "Just keep walking," the man said. "I'll tell you when to turn."

They walked in darkness for five minutes. When the lights went back on—how could he have seen to lead them?—Leia was thoroughly lost.

Whatever fat spider crouched in the center of this web, he truly did not want anybody just dropping by unannounced.

Eventually their driver led them into a hallway. At the end of the hall were two tall, carved wooden doors and, standing to the side, two more guards. These didn't wear armor and had no rifles but wore blasters on low-slung belts. One of them reached for the doorknob and opened it as they approached.

The driver said, "In there." With that, he turned and walked away.

Leia looked at Chewie. She realized her pulse was racing and her stomach was fluttery. She took a deep breath and let part of it out. She stepped into the room, Chewie behind her.

A tall man—no, not a man but an exotic-looking alien—rose from behind a large desk and smiled at her.

"Ah," he said, "Princess Leia Organa and Chewbacca. Welcome. I am Xizor."

Here she was at last, facing the person in charge of the galaxy's largest criminal organization. Perhaps now she would find out who wanted Luke dead, and why.

13

Xizor was pleased. The young woman sitting across from him, flanked by her furry bodyguard, would be every bit as helpful to him as he expected. Thus far they had spoken of trivial things. He pretended to be honored that she was a high Alliance official come to call; she pretended that she wasn't disgusted that he was a criminal. But, in fact, it didn't really matter what she felt, now that she was in his grasp.

No, now she would begin to feel only what he allowed her to feel. Already he had allowed some of the biochemicals in his skin to seep into the air. The Wookiee didn't seem to notice, but Princess Leia had already begun to respond to the chemical attractants. He knew that by now she would have begun to feel drawn toward him, to feel as if he were truly a good man, one to be trusted.

"You must be tired from your trip," Xizor said. "You should relax a bit before we discuss serious matters. I'll have my servant, Howzmin, show you to your quarters. You will be provided with fresh clothes. Refresh yourself and rejoin me in a couple of hours."

Xizor made sure that his words did not include the Wookiee. The plans for Chewbacca were altogether different from those he had for Leia. But when taken together, they would add up to one thing: the death of Luke Skywalker.

One way or another.

Xizor smiled as the doors of his sanctum opened and Leia stood framed in the entrance. "Do come in, Princess. Something to drink? Luranian brandy? Green champagne?"

"Tea would be fine, Your Highness," Leia answered.

"Call me Xizor, please," he said. "We can dispense with titles now that we are alone."

Leia watched as Xizor poured her tea. He seemed almost to glow, and she felt dizzy watching him. She moved to the couch, sat on one end. She tried to relax but felt a strange tension grip her. Xizor handed her the teacup and sat on the other end of the couch.

He said, "So, the Alliance might be interested in doing business with Black Sun?" He sipped at whatever it was he was drinking.

Leia thought he looked absolutely fascinating as he drank.

She scrambled to collect her thoughts. "Uh, yes, we, that is to say, the Alliance, we have been considering such an alliance."

Alliance considering an alliance? What is the matter with you, Leia?

Xizor seemed to take no notice of her poor choice of language.

"Well, certainly there are advantages to such a . . . liaison," he said.

She shook her head, trying to clear it.

"I—We—The Alliance, we feel that while Black Sun's aims are not the same as ours, the Empire is our mutual enemy," she stammered.

"And the enemy of my enemy is my friend?" He smiled. "We are friends, aren't we, Leia?"

Friends . . . yes, Leia thought. They were friends, she and Xizor. She cared deeply for him. He was her best friend.

Something was wrong here. She felt too good. As if being here were the best thing in the universe.

Something was most definitely wrong.

In hyperspace, Vader considered his next move. He had arrived too late at the suspected Rebel base on the Kothlisian moon to collect Luke, but he had waved the Imperial flag and blown up a small spaceport. Whether or not the port had anything to do with the Rebels didn't matter, only that they thought he thought it did and thus reasoned that the computer they had stolen was important to the Empire.

Half his mission had been accomplished, though to his mind, it was the lesser half.

He had no evidence against Xizor, only speculation and rumor. Thirdhand knowledge by a failed bounty hunter would hardly be enough. He was convinced, but the Emperor would not be so easily swayed. He needed more before he could move against the Dark Prince.

Well. If there was more to be had, he would have it. Now that he knew what he was looking for.

14

Xizor smiled with pleasure when he was certain Princess Leia was completely under his spell. He had her now.

There was a pounding at the door.

What? Who dared?

Leia jumped, eyes wide with confusion. Somebody started braying outside. The pounding increased.

That blasted Wookiee! Why was he here?

Flustered, Leia said, "I—I'd better see what he wants."

"Stay. I'll get rid of him." Xizor started to rise.

"N-No, I'll do it."

Xizor smiled when he realized that she was still in his control. "As you wish."

He watched her get to her feet. She swayed a little as she walked to the door. This was only a temporary setback.

Leia touched the door controls—Xizor had locked them—and the door slid wide.

The Wookiee gargled at her. Xizor's command of the tongue was imperfect, but he managed to catch the gist of what the tall, furry creature said. He wanted Leia to come with him, now.

"I'm in the middle of a, a . . . delicate discussion here," she said. "Can't it wait?"

The Wookiee ranted some more. Maybe he was smarter than he looked; he knew something was going on that threatened her.

Leia turned and glanced at Xizor. "He seems upset," she said. "Maybe I better go and see what he wants?"

Now that he had her under his control, Xizor could do as he wished with her. "As you like. I'll be here."

He waved her away, unworried.

She'd be back.

In the hall outside Xizor's sanctum, Leia glared at Chewie, who glared right back at her. "This better be good!"

Howzmin lay on the floor in a heap—unconscious or dead, she couldn't tell which. Chewie grabbed her by the arm and hustled her down the hallway.

"Let go of me, you overgrown stuffed toy!"

Chewie paid her no mind. When they came to a small alcove a short distance away, Chewie shoved Leia into it and stepped in behind her.

"You are going to be sorry, you—"

He pressed one hairy hand over her mouth, pointed up at the ceiling with his other hand.

Leia looked. Saw a small parabolic microphone inset into the ceiling.

"Somebody is listening?" she whispered.

He nodded.

"Are we being watched, too?"

Chewie shook his head. That was why he'd brought her here, she realized. It must be a blind spot. He was protecting her.

In that moment, all the attraction she had felt toward Xizor evaporated. Xizor was a criminal—more likely than not, an enemy of the Alliance and everything Leia stood for. Was he using some kind of drug, in her tea, maybe? That would explain a lot.

And Luke?

Suddenly the knowledge came to her: It wasn't Vader who wanted Luke dead . . .

As Vader expected, the Emperor was not convinced by his claims regarding Prince Xizor.

"You disappoint me, Lord Vader. I sense that your judgment is shaded by something of a personal grudge here."

"No, my master. I am merely concerned about the criminal's treachery. If he is in fact trying to kill Skywalker . . ."

The Emperor cut him off. "Really, Lord Vader, I would certainly need more evidence than a rumor from some bounty hunter to move against so valuable an ally. Did he not give us that Rebel base? Has he not put his vast shipping fleet at our disposal?"

"I have not forgotten these things," Vader said. He tried to keep his voice steady and even. "But I have also not forgotten my promise to bring Skywalker to the dark side. Which will not be possible if he is slain before I can get to him."

"Young Skywalker has managed to stay alive this long. If he is as strong in the Force as we assume he is, he will continue to live until you find him, don't you think? But since it seems so important to you, I give you leave to search for Skywalker. For a short while, for there are other tasks I would have you perform. Is this satisfactory?"

"Yes, my master."

He did want to find his son, but he also had to build a case against Xizor. Either of these would command much of his attention alone. Both of them at the same time would be difficult.

But he was one with the dark side. He would manage.

Leia took a deep breath, blew half of it out, and opened the door to Xizor's chamber.

The head of Black Sun sat on the couch where she'd left him, the glass in his hand. He smiled. "I was beginning to worry about you."

She smiled, hoping it didn't look false. She could still feel the charisma he exuded, but now she could resist it.

Now she had to keep Xizor busy long enough to give Chewie a chance to escape, or at least to get a good start on it. Chewie hadn't liked the idea, but she had convinced him he could help her better if he could get away from here and get help.

"Come back and sit here next to me," Xizor said. It was not a request.

Instead Leia moved toward the bar. "Let me make myself some tea first," she said. "I seem to have gotten rather thirsty."

She took her time making the tea. When she was done, she sipped at it but made no move to approach him.

"Come here," he said. Definitely a command.

Leia put the tea down and started for him.

He smiled again. He thought he had her under his control.

"Sit down here, next to me," he said.

"No," she said.

He put the glass down and came to his feet. "What?"

"I have decided that it is not possible for the Alliance to negotiate with Black Sun at this time," she said.

"So. You resist me."

"You got that right," she said.

He shook his head. "I am pleased that you are a worthy adversary." He bowed. "Guri."

A panel slid aside in the wall behind him, and the droid stepped into the room.

"Take her to her room and lock her in," Xizor said to Guri. To Leia he said, "Sooner or later, I believe you'll find that I am not such bad company."

"Don't bet on it," she said.

Guri took Leia's arm. Her grip was like a steel clamp.

Leia hoped Chewie had gotten enough of a head start.

After Guri had taken Leia away, Xizor sipped at another glass of green champagne. After a while he called his chief of security.

"Did the Wookiee escape?" he asked.

"Yes, Highness."

"You did not allow him to think it was too easy?"

"He put five of our troops down, my prince," the chief replied. "We singed him with a blaster beam as he ran down a hall. He won't think it was easy."

"Good."

Xizor broke the link and smiled into the green, bubbly liquid. He had intended to let the Wookiee go all along, although not quite this soon. *Well. No matter.* The Wookiee would surely contact Skywalker, and the boy would come running to try to rescue the princess. Xizor's agents would probably collect Skywalker before he got within hours of the castle.

So easy.

A priority offworld message announced itself on his private channel. "Yes?"

"My prince, there is news of Skywalker. He was captured by a group of bounty hunters and taken to Kothlis. There is a problem, however."

"I see. And this problem is . . . ?"

"It—It seems that Skywalker has escaped custody. And Darth Vader is now personally involved. He was seen near the site of the escape within hours of the event."

Xizor laughed.

"M-My prince?"

Finally, some good news. Vader had just missed Skywalker. The boy was free, and as long as Leia was safely installed here, sooner or later Skywalker would show up on Xizor's doorstep.

The Wookiee would see to that.

Lando didn't want to stop, but Luke insisted. Lando still wouldn't tell him where Leia was, and Luke felt something was wrong.

"Look, I trust the Force and it's telling me Leia is in danger. So let's just put in a call and check, okay?" Luke urged.

"Can't it wait until we get to Tatooine?"

"No," Luke said firmly.

Lando sighed. "All right. But remember I did this. You owe me one."

He dropped the *Falcon* out of hyperspace. There was a system not far away, and Lando headed for it. They had to find a place to make the call.

It didn't take long. There was a repair station on a small moon with a public comm unit. Lando broke into the unit with a stolen override card, and the call went against the Empire's bill. Luke called the number Lando gave him for Dash while the gambler kept fiddling with the override to make sure the communication wasn't tapped.

Dash didn't answer, but there was a message loop.

Luke turned to Lando. "Do we have the 'play message' code?"

"Yes." Lando gave it to him.

The image that ghosted into being surprised them. A

105

Wookiee with a bad haircut. Luke didn't recognize him at first. Until he started talking. Yelling was more like it.

Chewie!

"What!" Lando said.

"What is it?" Luke asked, filled with dread.

Lando translated. "Leia is being held at Imperial Center by Black Sun. They tried to kill Chewie, but he escaped—the princess made him go, it wasn't his idea . . ."

Abruptly the transmission ended.

"Let's go," Luke said.

"To Tatooine, right?"

"Wrong."

"Somehow I knew you were gonna say that," Lando said, and sighed.

15

"I really don't think this is a good idea, Master Luke. I believe it would be much better if Artoo and I went with you and Master Lando."

Artoo cheeped his agreement.

"Look, you'll be fine here on the ship," Luke said. "We need you here in case we need help. Besides, it'll be a lot more dangerous out there than in here."

"Ah. Well, in that case, perhaps we should stay here."

Artoo cheeped.

"No, you heard Master Luke, he needs us on the ship in case anything goes wrong."

"Wrong, what could possibly go wrong?" Lando said. "Just because we've got huge rewards posted everywhere in the galaxy for us, dead or alive, and we've plunked ourselves down smack in the black and evil heart of the Empire?"

Luke shook his head. "Come on. Where would be the last place you'd look for us if you were an Imperial operative or a bounty hunter?"

"Yeah, I guess you're right. They'd figure nobody would be that stupid. Lucky for us they don't know we *are* that stupid."

Luke shook his head. All this banter was an attempt to make light of the situation. The truth was, this was dangerous. To Threepio he said in a more serious voice, "Look, I'll be honest. There's a good chance we won't make it back. If that happens, don't call the Alliance for help. There's no point in putting any part of the fleet in jeopardy."

Threepio said, "I understand."

Artoo whistled and cheeped rapidly. The tone was upset.

Luke looked at the little droid. He squatted down and laid one hand on Artoo's dome. "Just stand by the comm, okay? We'll call you if we need you. If we get in trouble, you can try to come and get us. Threepio has the hands and feet, you have the astronavigational skills. I'm sure the two of you working together can fly the *Falcon* in an emergency."

Luke and Lando left the old warehouse where a 'business associate' of Lando's had allowed them to hide the *Millennium Falcon*. Now they had to find a way into Black Sun's stronghold.

Xizor was in his bath, a sunken tub carved from dense black garden stone. Here was a place where he allowed himself to relax totally. He would sometimes have music piped in, when the mood struck him, but he wanted nothing else to intrude on his peace while he soaked away the day's tensions.

Guri strode into the bathroom and stopped next to the tub.

She produced a small comlink. "The Emperor," she said.

Xizor sat up and grabbed the comlink. "My master," he said.

"I shall be leaving the planet shortly," the Emperor continued. "To inspect portions of a certain . . . construction project of which you are aware. When I return, we must get together. I have a few things I would like to discuss with you."

"Of course, my master."

"Tales have reached me concerning one of the Rebels, Luke Skywalker. It seems you have an interest in him?"

"Skywalker? I have heard the name. I cannot say I have an interest in him," Xizor said guardedly.

"We shall speak of this on my return."

The conversation over, the Emperor disconnected.

Xizor put the small comlink cylinder on the edge of the tub and allowed himself to sink deeper into the tranquilizing water. *Well.* It was to be expected that the Emperor would find out about his plans sooner or later. It affected nothing, as long as Xizor remained cautious.

Rumors were not proof.

Luke and Lando were in a maglev train station not far below the surface of Imperial Center. The waiting platform was crowded, and there were Imperial stormtroopers in armor and uniformed officers circulating in the huge room.

"I think maybe it's time we got some disguises," Lando said.

"What did you have in mind?"

"Ideally, we want to look like somebody nobody'll pay any attention to."

"Stormtroopers?"

Lando nodded. "Yeah. Or maybe the Elite Stormtroopers would be better. Their faces are covered, and since they're so well regarded, nobody is apt to bother them."

Luke looked around. "I see one about my size, over there by the ticket droid."

"Yep, and there's one about my height and weight, by the periodical dispenser. Maybe we should do our duty to the Empire and report something strange going on in one of the 'fresher booths, you think?"

"Just as any loyal citizen would," Luke said.

He and Lando grinned at each other.

Vader stood at the ramp leading to the Emperor's personal shuttle, looking down at the shorter man.

"I anticipate that I shall return in three weeks," the Emperor told him. "I trust you can keep the planet from falling apart while I am gone?"

"Yes, my master."

"I expect no less. Any news of Skywalker?"

"Not yet. We'll find him," Vader vowed.

"Perhaps sooner than you expect."

"Well," Luke said, "this is a better neighborhood than where we were before, but where exactly are we going?"

Lando pointed. "There." Both he and Luke were now

disguised as Elite Stormtroopers, having "obtained" uniforms from the two guards they had spotted.

"A plant shop?" Luke asked.

"Don't let it fool you. It's run by an old Ho'Din, name of Spero. He's got a lot of connections, some Imperial, some Alliance, some criminal."

"Let me guess: He owes you a favor."

"Not exactly. But we've done some business in the past, and he doesn't mind making a few credits passing along information."

Inside the shop there was no sign of the Ho'Din owner. Except for Luke and Lando, the place was empty.

"Nobody home," Luke said. "That's odd, isn't it?"

"Yeah, odd. I—"

Somebody said something behind them. Luke didn't understand what it was, but he recognized the language: Wookiee.

"Easy, friend," Lando said. "Nobody is going to make any sudden moves." He lifted his hands away from his body, told Luke to do the same.

The Wookiee speaker said something else.

Something about the voice . . .

"Turn around, nice and slow," Lando told Luke.

They turned.

"Chewie!" Lando said.

Despite the stormtrooper helmets, Chewbacca recognized them and lowered the blaster pistol he held.

Lando smiled as he and Luke moved forward to embrace Chewie.

"What happened?"

Chewie tried to answer at the same time Lando fired more questions, and Luke didn't get much of it. But he was glad to see the Wookiee.

Finally Lando began to translate for Luke.

"The shop owner is tied up in back, in case anybody spotted Chewie coming in, so they wouldn't think the Ho'Din was helping, right, right, and slow down, pal!"

Chewie kept talking.

"Okay, okay, Leia thinks it's Black Sun that wants you dead, Luke, they're behind the assassination attempts, not the Empire. Huh? Well, I don't know how."

The talk ended abruptly as a blaster bolt lanced through the shop's open door and shattered a flowerpot hanging from the ceiling. Shards of the ceramic pattered against Luke's back, and clumps of moist dirt fell around him.

Outside the shop were four men with blasters. They weren't wearing uniforms, whoever they were.

The three inside the plant store dropped to the floor. Chewie raised his blaster and fired several rounds blindly back at the shooters.

"Who are those guys? Why are they shooting at us?"

Lando said, "How do I know!" He pulled his borrowed blaster and added to Chewie's return fire. From the torrent of light that came back at them, it didn't look as if they'd hit anybody.

"Is there another way out of here?" Luke asked.

Chewie growled a reply.

"In the back!" Lando yelled.

He and Chewie cooked off several more shots, and the three of them crawled toward the back of the shop.

They passed an old Ho'Din bound and gagged in a corner.

"Sorry about this," Lando said to the Ho'Din. "Send the Alliance a bill, they'll pay for it!"

Chewie reached the back exit and shoved the sliding door open.

Another high-energy bolt zipped through the door at chest height and burned a hole in an inner wall. Fortunately, they were all still stretched out on the floor and it was well above their heads.

Lando yelled. "They've got us boxed!"

Before they could think about what they were going to do, somebody outside the back exit screamed. There came the sound of several blaster discharges—but no fresh beams poked into the shop.

"What the . . . ?" Lando began.

Luke looked up from where he lay on the floor, and saw a figure walking across the alley. Well, not walking so much as . . . swaggering.

Dash Rendar! Oh, man. Dash was saving Luke again. He hated this.

"Howdy, boys. Having a little trouble?" Dash spun his blaster on his forefinger and blew across the end of the barrel.

Luke got up and started to speak, but Lando beat him to it. "Rendar! What are you doing here?"

"Saving your butts, looks like. Seems to be my specialty. Better come on, we can talk as we move. Follow me."

Dash showed the way. Chewie took the point and led them into a warren of twisted corridors and tunnels that would lose any pursuers.

"So how did you get here?" Lando asked Dash.

"The usual way. Sneaked in under the belly of a freighter in the sensor shadow. A trick I learned as a boy at the Academy."

"Yeah, but how did you manage to get *here*?" Luke asked. He pointed at the ground.

"The Ho'Din's? Oh, everybody knows about Spero, don't they, Lando?"

"I guess they do," Lando said. "Okay, that's how, but why?"

Dash sighed. "Something to prove, I guess. I felt pretty bad after that disaster Luke and I went through. Not something I'm used to, making mistakes. I work for money, but I figure I owe the Empire a little something. When Chewie called, I decided it was time to pay the Empire back."

Luke nodded. "I understand how you feel."

Guri stood in front of Xizor as he dressed for his day's business appointments.

"Our agents say that a Corellian freighter answering the description of the *Millennium Falcon* is hidden somewhere in the Hasamadhi warehouse district near the South Pole," she reported.

Xizor selected a tunic and matching pants from the

closet and examined them under the artificial sunlight. "So? There are hundreds of Corellian freighters that look like that, are there not?"

"Not hidden in the Hasamadhi warehouse district."

"All right. Check it out. If it is Skywalker's ship, have it watched. When he shows up, have our people kill him."

She nodded, turned, and left.

Xizor didn't really expect Skywalker to have arrived here so soon, but it was possible. If it *was* him, so much the better. Vader would be made to look a fool by having Skywalker killed under his very nose. Things could hardly be moving along any more smoothly, could they?

16

She was using the computer, trying to find a floor plan for Xizor's castle. He wasn't foolish enough to leave one where she could access it—too bad.

Leia . . .

Since it had happened before, on Bespin, she recognized the sensation quickly.

Luke.

She took a deep breath, let part of it out, and held her silence. She was being watched, and she must give no sign of the connection with Luke. She pretended to look at whatever the computer image was, but she was seeing through it, into the distance beyond it, beyond the walls.

Leia, I'm here, I'm coming for you.

That was what Luke was saying, if she could have put it into words. But it wasn't expressed in words; it was a feeling, and she felt the truth of it.

Luke was here, in Imperial Center, not far away. He was coming for her. There was a calmness about him she hadn't felt before. He had grown stronger; his control of the Force was better. Maybe he could rescue her. Maybe they would survive all this somehow.

Leia . . .

She smiled. *Luke. I'm here* . . .

Luke Skywalker, Jedi Knight, smiled.

In his chamber, Darth Vader felt the ripple in the Force.

Luke. He was here. In Imperial Center. The knowledge sent a chill through Vader's body.

He reached out, tried to touch his son: Luke . . .

He frowned. The way was blocked. It was as if Luke's power had not only increased, it seemed to be in two separate places.

Impossible. He was interpreting the energies wrong. There could be no one else as strong as Luke in the Force. The Jedi were all dead. The Emperor was light-years away.

What could be causing that echo effect? Surely that was all it was, an echo, some reverberation in the Force.

After a moment the ripple passed and Vader was alone again. But he knew for certain that Luke was here. He would find him. Find him—and bring him to the dark side.

They sat at a small table in the Underground hotel's restaurant, waiting for their meal to be served.

Dash began. "This is the center of the Empire—"

"It is?" Lando cut in. "Uh-oh. We shouldn't be here. Why, it could be . . . dangerous."

"What's your point, Dash?" Luke asked, ignoring Lando's sarcasm.

"The Empire is corrupt. It runs less on loyalty and honor than it does on bribes and graft," Dash explained.

"So? You think we're going to be able to bribe a guard? I don't think Black Sun is likely to put those kind of people on the door," Lando said.

"Not a guard, an engineer."

"What am I missing here?" Luke asked.

Dash continued. "In a bureaucracy, everything has to be filed and copied and logged in quadruplicate. You can't build anything without permits, licenses, inspections, plans. We know that the really big buildings on this planet extend as far under the surface as they do above it. Sewage has to be pumped away where bigger and more efficient systems can work on it."

"So?" Luke said.

"A building as big as this one"—here he tapped a holographic postcard showing several huge structures, including the Emperor's castle—"generates a lot of waste. There has to be a way to get rid of it. I haven't seen any garbage vans or drain wagons on the streets or in the skies of Imperial Center, so they have to break the solid waste down and pump it away. Therefore we are talking about pipes."

Luke got it. He looked around the table. "Big pipes."

Chewie said something.

Lando nodded, and said, "Chewie is right. Those pipes, if they are big enough to admit people, will certainly be guarded."

Chewie said something else.

"Yeah," Dash said. "Chewie also points out such drains would be hard to locate, given that every building will have similar systems. It's probably a monster maze under the ground."

Dash continued. "But there will probably be fewer guards posted on a big sewage drain than the doors aboveground. They wouldn't really expect any kind of assault that way. You couldn't move a lot of troops in without making noise their sensors would pick up. But a few men could be lost in the background gurgle, if they were careful."

Lando looked at Luke and Chewie, then back at Dash. "Assuming we could find a guide, are you saying you want us to wade through kilometers of sewage to get into this place?"

Dash smiled. "Exactly what the guards would think. Who would be that stupid?"

Lando shook his head. "Us. Who else?"

"And finding a guide is no problem. I know somebody."

"I've heard that before," Luke said.

17

"Threepio? Everything okay on the ship?"

There was a short pause. Luke twirled the small comlink absently in his fingers.

Threepio's voice was somewhat tinny from the comlink. "On the ship, yes. But Artoo has overheard some tactical communications on a shielded operations channel. Apparently there are search teams in the area. They seem to be looking for a Corellian freighter."

Luke stared at the comlink. "Hmm. Okay. Keep a sharp eye out. If anybody starts snooping around you, call me."

"Certainly I shall. Right away," Threepio said.

Luke chewed at his lip. They were about to go into the sewers with Benedict Vidkun, the engineer Dash had found. He didn't need any more problems.

Vader stood on the balcony of his castle, immune to the night breeze that washed over him. He had tried to reach out with the Force and find Luke but had failed. Surely it was Luke? Who else could it be? And if it was—where he was exactly was probably not as important as why he was here in the Imperial Center.

Vader turned. A little man who had previously supplied him with damaging information about Xizor stood there. Vader had left orders he was to be admitted no matter when he arrived.

"You have something new for me?"

"Yes, my lord. We have uncovered a pirated copy of some of the planetary files for Falleen, thought to be destroyed. It contains some material about Prince Xizor's family. His father was king of a small nation there," the agent began.

Vader frowned. "I knew his father was royalty, but I have been given to understand that Prince Xizor was orphaned at an early age."

"Not precisely, my lord. You may recall a biological experiment on Falleen that . . . went awry a decade or so past."

"Yes, I recall."

"During the, ah, sterilization procedure, some Imperial citizens' lives were lost," the agent explained.

"A regrettable incident," Vader said sincerely.

"All of Prince Xizor's family was killed during the destruction of the mutant bacterium that escaped from the lab," the little man said.

A light dawned then, bright and clear and sudden in Vader's mind. *Ah!* That explained much. It was not simply that Xizor considered Vader a competitor for the Emperor's affection, a roadblock to his ambitions.

It was personal.

"How did the records of this come to be destroyed?" Vader asked.

The little man shook his head. "We do not know. For some reason, all references to Xizor's family simply vanished, shortly after the destruction of the city."

Darth Vader had been in charge of that project. Xizor must consider him responsible for the deaths of his family. And now he wanted to kill Luke—Vader's son. Not simply to make him lose face in the eyes of the Emperor, but for revenge!

It made sense. Through Black Sun, Xizor had the means to eliminate the records. He was Falleen and thus patient. Was it not the Falleen who said that vengeance was like fine wine? It should be aged until it was perfect. They were cold, the lizard men, they could wait for a long time to get what they wanted.

Well. So could he.

By the time they were ready to leave, the small band was outfitted with all the gear they thought they might need for a long hike through the sewers followed by an assault on a heavily fortified building.

Luke certainly didn't consider himself a Jedi Knight, but he elected to use his lightsaber as a weapon. Chewie managed to locate a bowcaster, and Lando and Dash stuck to their own blasters. Nobody offered Vidkun a weapon—if the shooting started, they weren't at all sure which way he might be firing.

Dash had expressed it by saying that people like Vidkun were useful—but you didn't trust them any farther than you could see them. You paid them what you owed and then got as far away as you could, fast.

They elected to go during daylight. Vidkun would normally be off work and thus would not be missed. That far under the ground, it wouldn't matter what the sun was doing, either.

Luke shifted some of the gear on his belt and adjusted the small backpack so that it rode more comfortably on his shoulders.

"Ready?" Dash asked.

Everybody was.

"Let's do it."

In his sanctum, Xizor was mildly surprised at the incoming call.

"Lord Vader. What a pleasant surprise."

When Vader spoke, the steel in his voice was barely covered by a thin layer of civility. "Perhaps not so pleasant. I have been made aware of your attempts to kill Luke Skywalker. You will cease all attempts to harm the boy immediately."

Xizor kept his face neutral, though he felt a violent surge of anger. "Your information is in error, Lord Vader. And even if it were correct, I am given to understand that the boy is a Rebel officer, all of whom are traitors and wanted dead or alive. Is this sudden change of policy an official Imperial decree?"

"If Skywalker is harmed, I will hold you personally accountable."

"I see. I assure you that if I should happen to come across Skywalker, I will extend to him the same courtesy I would to you, Lord Vader."

Vader broke the connection.

Xizor took a deep breath and exhaled slowly. Again he told himself it was to be expected that Vader, as had the Emperor, would uncover some information about Skywalker sooner or later. Few things of any real value could be kept secret forever.

This conversation was mildly upsetting, nothing more, and in fact had given Xizor knowledge he had not had before. Vader was not sleeping, and that was good to know.

Underestimating one's enemy was always a bad thing.

18

The sludge was greenish black, thick, and oily, and it stank worse than anything Luke had ever smelled before. The silty goop flowed around their feet, sloshing sometimes deeper than their ankles. Luke was very glad he was wearing calf-length boots with his new clothes.

The tunnel in which they walked was as big as Vidkun had promised. It was lighted by a row of somewhat dim overhead glowsticks but bright enough for them to see as much as they needed.

The five of them continued to wade through the mire.

"Just ahead, there," Vidkun said.

They stopped. There were two large round holes in the wall, covered with finger-thick metal mesh gates. The holes were angled down slightly.

Lando said, "Okay, Vidkun, let's see if those codes you have work."

The engineer moved forward and did something to the locking mechanisms with a plastic card. The gates swung open. He grinned at them. "See? Just like I told you. We want the one on the right."

They moved into the drain and climbed the slight incline very carefully.

You'd think that after a while you'd get used to the smell, Luke thought. But it seemed to grow constantly worse, bringing forth stinks he'd never imagined. It was going to take a really hot, really long shower to wash the stench off.

"Not far now," the engineer said.

"Good," Lando, Luke, and Dash all said together. Chewie said something, too, and Luke didn't need a translator to figure out he was in agreement. Better to face Xizor's guards than endure this guck much longer.

"There," Vidkun whispered. "There is the entrance to the building. It leads into the recycler in the sub-sub-basement. There won't be any guards inside the recycler itself, but there will probably be some in the adjoining flow chamber. Here's the key to the rat-grate." He handed a plastic card to Lando. "See you."

He turned to leave.

Dash stepped in front of him. "Where do you think you're going?"

"Hey, I'm done. I got you to the building, I got you the floor plans for the place, that was the deal."

"Well, I guess you have us there," Dash said. "That was the deal, all right. But see, there's been a little change in our itinerary."

Vidkun looked alarmed.

"Easy. We aren't going to blast you or anything. We'd just like you to come along until we get to a place where you can safely wait for us."

Vidkun wasn't having any of it. "No offense or anything, but what if you get killed? I might be waiting a long time!"

"I guess you'll have to take that chance," Lando said. "It's not that we don't trust you. It's just that we don't trust you. We insist." He patted his blaster.

Vidkun shrugged. "Well, okay. Since you put it that way . . ."

And before anybody could react, he pulled a small blaster of his own from his coverall and started shooting wildly.

Luke hadn't seen it coming. He was slow to clear his lightsaber.

The first shot seared past, a clean miss.

The second shot hit Dash. Luke heard him grunt.

The engineer didn't get off a third shot because Dash snapped his blaster up and put a bolt right between the man's eyes. Vidkun went down with a gooey splash that sprayed black onto the tunnel walls.

"Dash?"

"I'm okay. Just scorched me a little."

Dash turned and showed the burn along his left hip. The bolt had sliced a clean line of his coverall away and raised a large blister. It wasn't even bleeding.

"Don't get any of this crud on you," Lando said, waving at the sewage. "Probably wouldn't do you any good."

"Where'd he get the blaster?" Luke said, replacing his lightsaber.

"Must have had it all along," Lando said. "What I'm wondering is, why'd he do it? We weren't going to hurt him."

"Guy like that, he figures he sold out, why shouldn't we?" Dash said.

Luke opened the first aid kit he'd brought and offered Dash a surgical dressing. Dash slapped the patch on over his hip, pressed the seal, and relaxed a little as the topical painkiller in the bandage coated the wound.

"Let's hope the guards didn't hear the shooting," Lando said.

"Yeah." Luke looked around, took a deep breath. "Ready?"

They were.

"Uh-oh," Luke whispered.

Crouched behind him in the recycler, Lando whispered back, "I do not need to hear that. What is it?"

"Guards," Luke said.

"So?"

"There are six of them."

"Six? To guard a sewage plant?"

"So what?" Dash whispered. "That's only one and a half each. How long does it take you to pull a trigger, Calrissian?"

"Shhh!" Luke said. He peered through the half-fogged cover plate on the recycler's door again. There were six men only a few meters away. Four of them sat at a table, playing cards, blast rifles stacked against the wall. Two others stood near the cardplayers, watching and apparently offering advice. They had their weapons slung over their shoulders. Dash was right. If they moved fast, they could cover the guards before they had a chance to unship their rifles. The trick was to do it before one of the guards got his comlink out to call for help.

"Okay. Ready?" Luke held the lightsaber down low so that the glow wouldn't give them away and clicked it on. He took a couple of deep breaths.

"On three. One . . . two . . . three!"

Dash shoved the hatch open.

Luke leaped out, brought his lightsaber up into a ready stance.

"Nobody move!" he yelled.

Chewie jumped out behind him. The Wookiee's wet feet slid on the floor as if he were wearing ice skates, and he fell flat on his back. Lando tried to leap over Chewie but tripped and sprawled facedown.

The guards weren't slow. The two standing unslung their blast rifles, swung them up, and fired.

Luke blocked the first bolt, shifted in the Force, and blocked the second.

Dash dived over Lando and Chewie, shoulder-rolled once, stretched out prone, and fired, once, twice, three times. The two standing guards went down, but another one spun away from the wall, blast rifle spewing.

Dash's blaster spat hard light again and again. The guards were all down now save one, but he didn't have a gun. He was yelling into a comlink.

Lando shot the last guard, and he dropped. The comlink flew from his hand and rolled to a stop next to Luke's boots.

From the comlink came a tinny voice: "Thix? What is going on down there? Thix? Come in, sector one-one-three-eight, come in—"

Chewie got to his feet. The Wookiee shrugged and looked embarrassed. Luke shook his head. He stomped down on the squawking comlink with his boot heel and smashed it.

"So much for sneaking in quietly," Lando said.

Xizor was paying the cultural minister his monthly bribe when Guri stepped into the room. The Dark Prince dismissed the minister.

When the man was gone, he said, "What?"

"A problem in the sub-subbasement."

"What kind of problem?" Xizor snapped.

She shrugged. "We don't know. That area is still not wired for surveillance, and the guards are not answering."

"It's either a comm glitch—or Skywalker is faster and smarter than we thought. Have the drain sensors picked up any armies marching in under the building?" he asked.

"No."

"Good. If it is Skywalker, he's probably alone, or perhaps the Wookiee is with him. Send a unit to check it out."

"Two squads are already on the way," she said.

Luke and the others ran. Chewie knew where Leia was, so he was in the lead. They came around a sharp corner in a wide corridor and nearly ran into four more guards. Everybody who had a blaster started shooting. From the comlink on Luke's belt, Threepio's strident and excited voice suddenly began calling:

"Master Luke, Master Luke!"

Luke blocked an incoming blaster beam. He yelled at the comlink but left it on his belt: "We're busy here, Threepio!"

"But Master Luke, there are men coming toward the ship! Men with guns!" Threepio screeched in panic.

Great. Just what they needed.

Luke deflected another beam, leaped forward, and found himself within reach of the man who'd shot at him. He whipped the lightsaber down, and the hand holding the blaster dropped to the floor. Luke spun and thrust a side kick at the guard, hit him squarely on the nose, and knocked him flat.

The other guards were all down as well. Luke pointed the way the guards had just come. "That way—it ought to be clear!"

As they ran, he pulled his comlink from his belt. "Threepio?"

"Master Luke. Oh, what shall we do?"

"Take the ship out of there, now! Just like we talked about. Artoo knows the systems; you can operate the controls. Call me back when you're in the air. Keep it suborbital and under the stratospheric security scanners, you got that?"

"Yes, Master Luke!"

"Go!"

Leia felt something in the air. A sense of impending . . . something she couldn't quite touch.

Luke. Luke was here.

She began to gather the parts of her disguise.

"We've lost contact with the second unit of guards," Guri told Xizor.

"Same area?" he asked.

"No. Four levels up."

"Put security on full alert."

"Already done," she said.

Could it be Skywalker? Had he somehow gotten into the castle without being detected? Or was it someone else?

"Cancel my appointments," Xizor ordered. "Go and fetch Princess Leia. Bring her to my strong room."

Chewie led them up another eight or ten floors before they ran into more guards. The exchange of blaster fire was fast, the air full of crackling energy, shouting, and the smell of burned wall and ozone.

Dash was right about one thing: He could shoot. He nailed three guards with three shots—*zap, zap, zap!*—as fast as anybody Luke had ever seen. Luke himself deflected or blocked the bolts that came his way, the ricochets adding to the general confusion. Chewie and Lando pounded away with their weapons. The guards were not bad, but they weren't desperate. They were shooting for pay. Luke and his friends were shooting for their lives. The last guard standing turned and ran. Chewie spiked him, and he did a belly-flop onto the floor and skidded two meters before veering into a side wall and thumping to a halt.

"Go, go, go!"

Leia felt somebody approaching her room. Intuition, but she trusted it. She grabbed one of the chairs and slid it next to the door. She stood on the back of it and balanced carefully against the wall, clutching the heavy bounty hunter's helmet tightly in her hands.

The door opened, and Guri stepped into the room. She was fast, but Leia had already started moving. Before Guri could turn, Leia hammered the back of her head with the helmet. It was a powerful blow and would have knocked a human unconscious. As it was, the impact was enough to put the droid off-balance, and she stumbled forward.

Leia leaped from the chair and scooted out of the room into the hall. She slapped the door control. Guri had recovered and was on the way back when the door shut. Leia jammed the lock mechanism closed.

The door shook from Guri's impact.

The next hit splintered the heavy plastic, spiderwebbing it with tiny cracks. It wasn't going to hold her long, Leia knew.

She turned and ran.

Chewie led them up a stairwell a dozen levels above where they'd entered the castle.

"Master Luke? We have successfully left the building," Threepio reported over the comlink.

Luke pulled his comlink so that he wouldn't have to yell at it. "Where are you?"

"Somewhere in the sky, Master Luke, I—what? Oh, be quiet, I'm flying it correctly, it—ah! Ahh!"

"Threepio?"

There was a moment of silence. Then a crunching noise. "I saw it, you blithering ashcan! If you hadn't distracted me I would have turned in time."

"Threepio, listen. Bring the *Falcon* to the coordinates I told you. Hurry. And gain enough altitude so you don't hit anything."

"Yes, Master Luke. We are on the way."

Luke had to break the connection then. There was a door just ahead of them, a heavy fireproof door, and it was locked.

Lando leveled his blaster at it, but Luke stopped him. "Don't. It's magnetically shielded. That will bounce off and maybe hit one of us."

"How are we supposed to get through it, then?" Lando asked.

"Stand back. Let's see if it will stop a lightsaber."

He lit the blade.

The door would not stop a lightsaber.

They went through and continued to climb.

Guri burst into Xizor's strong room. He blinked at her. "What?"

"She got away. She was waiting when I got there. She struck me from behind. I am undamaged, but it gave her enough time to slip out."

"Blast!" Xizor could not restrain himself. This was not good. This was his castle, and things were getting out of control. Had he underestimated Skywalker? Apparently so. Time to correct that.

He moved to a desk, opened a sliding panel, and removed from the hidden compartment a sleek, high-powered blaster.

"All right. Let's go find her. And whoever is causing these problems."

"This way!" Luke yelled.

Firing behind them, the four of them ran, blaster bolts stabbing after them.

They rounded another corner, zigzagged through a side corridor, and sprinted toward a door at the end of the hall. Heard somebody pounding toward the other side, saw the door start to slide back. Dash and Lando brought their guns up.

"No!" Luke yelled. "Don't shoot!"

The door opened wide to reveal . . .

"Leia!"

He ran to her. They embraced.

"Took you long enough," she said. She looked closer at them, wrinkled her nose. "Gah, what have you been swimming in?"

"We had to take a shortcut through the sewer."

"Never mind. Let's get out of here," Leia said. They ran.

"Master Luke?"

"What is it now, Threepio?"

135

"We appear to have caught the attention of a robotic police vessel. It seems to be following us."

"Well, lose it," Luke said simply.

"How, Master Luke?" Threepio pleaded.

"Fly like Han does."

Running next to him, Leia's eyes went wide. "You're letting the droids fly the ship? Are you crazy?"

"They're doing all right. Just a few jitters, that's all."

"We seem to have lost the pursuer, Master Luke. I believe it smashed into that walkway we flew under while we were upside down."

"I can't believe you let the droids fly the—"

Luke glared at her. "Will you stop saying that?" He looked back at the comlink. "All right, you two get to the coordinates like I said. And be more careful."

"We're doing quite well now, Master Luke. Don't worry."

Luke stared up at the ceiling and sighed.

19

"Security reports they're on the seventeenth floor," Guri said.

"Let's move, then," Xizor ordered.

"We don't know how many of them there are," Guri said. "We've lost at least a dozen guards. It is too dangerous for you to go there."

"I will be the judge of what is too dangerous," he said. "And since we know it is Skywalker, this is where it ends. I will dispatch him personally!"

He would not be embarrassed in his own castle.

"So what . . . is . . . the plan?" Leia said, breathless.

"We get out of here," Luke said. "Get to the *Falcon* and get offworld as fast as we can. Threepio and Artoo can do it."

She shook her head.

"Listen," Luke said, "nobody will think we're stupid enough to go up. They'll look for us to try and leave at ground level."

Lando laughed. "Yeah, that's the problem with our opposition—they keep thinking nobody could possibly be as stupid as we are. Fools 'em every time."

Xizor and Guri stepped into the turbolift. "Level twenty," Xizor ordered. "We'll wait for them there."

The turbolift dropped, giving him a moment of free fall that fluttered in his belly like a trapped bird trying to escape. Despite the anger he felt at being invaded, there was a sense of excitement about all this. It wasn't very often he got to dispatch people with his own hands. He was certain that the castle-breakers included Luke Skywalker. After his recent conversation with Vader and for daring to get this far, he would take particular pleasure in killing the boy.

The turbolift slowed. His weight seemed to increase as the floor of the lift pressed harder against the soles of his boots.

"Level twenty," the turbolift announced.

The door slid wide.

Xizor raised the blaster to point at the ceiling next to his right ear in a ready carry position. He spent a few hours a week practicing at his personal firing range. He was an excellent shot.

They stepped out into the corridor.

"Level twenty," Dash said. "Stairs end here, we'll have to zip in and find another set."

"How many levels are in this place?" Leia asked.

"As I recall, a hundred and two aboveground," Dash answered.

"Oh, man," Lando said. "And we have to go all the way to the roof?"

"No, there's a landing pad extending out from level fifty," Luke said.

"That's nothing. Another thirty flights, we won't even be breathing hard," Dash said.

"I can barely breathe now," Lando said.

"You're getting old, Calrissian."

"Yeah, and I'd like to get a lot older, too."

"There should be another set of stairs across the hall and down about sixty meters," Luke said. "Let's move."

Xizor saw them first because Guri was opening a side door, looking to see if they were already there and hiding. Five of them, Leia included. And Skywalker.

The Dark Prince smiled. He turned sideways, lowered his blaster, and extended it one-handed, his free hand on his opposite hip, just as if he were shooting targets in competition. He lined his sights up on Skywalker's left eye, let out half his breath, held it, squeezed the trigger gently . . .

Luke spotted the tall alien just as he pointed his blaster at him.

Luke jerked his lightsaber from his belt, flicked it on, and let the Force claim him. The deadly lance of energy rocketed at Luke. His lightsaber came across and stopped itself in front of his face, blocking the view from his left eye.

He felt the impact as the energy of his blade deflected the energy of the incoming bolt. It would have hit him right in the eye.

The alien fired again.

Again the lightsaber moved, directed by the Force. Another beam splashed harmlessly against the handmade Jedi weapon, bounced back and down, hit the floor, and burned through.

Xizor frowned. How could he do that? He couldn't be that fast!

He fired again.

Guri leaped out into the corridor. She held a chair, a heavy metal thing with casters on the bottom. She hurled it down the hallway as if it weighed no more than a pebble.

"Look out!" Luke yelled.

A chair pinwheeled at him. He couldn't use his saber to cut it down without risking another bolt from the shooter. Chewie stepped forward, level with Luke, brought his bowcaster up, and fired.

The chair exploded into shrapnel and sprayed them with a prickly hail.

Xizor realized two things: that he was outgunned and that Skywalker could stop his fire. He was more startled than afraid, but he knew he had to get out of the hall fast. "Move!" he yelled at Guri.

She stepped in front of him and blocked him from the five down the hall as he stepped into the empty room from which she'd gotten the chair. A second later Guri joined him.

"That's an interesting trick he does with that light-saber," Xizor observed.

"He is related to Vader," she said. "Shall I sound the general alarm?"

"Indeed," he said sternly. "Find out why security is taking so long."

She was already speaking into her comlink.

"That was Xizor!" Leia yelled.

"Good. Let's get him!" Luke yelled back.

"I don't think so," Lando said. "Look!"

A dozen guards rounded the end of the corridor and started shooting.

"In there!" Dash yelled.

There was a door to their left. Chewie opened it by smashing through it. Leia followed him, Lando and Dash behind her. Luke went last, blocking and batting aside beams that zipped at them like angry hornets.

Inside the room, some kind of office, they looked at each other.

"Now what?" Leia said.

Blaster bolts continued to whiz past the destroyed doorway.

Lando looked at Luke, who nodded. "Well," Lando said, "it's time for desperate measures." He reached into the small backpack he wore and came out with a round, silvery ball about the size of a man's fist. There were some controls, a fingerwide slot around the ball's equator, and what looked like electronic diodes on the top and in the slot.

Leia looked at the shiny ball, then at Luke. He nodded at Dash.

More blaster bolts sizzled past. They apparently hadn't noticed that nobody was shooting back.

Dash took the ball from Lando. "It's a thermal detonator," he said. "Lando's got three of them. They run on a timer or a deadman's switch. Flip that switch right there, press that button in, and hold it. If you let go without disarming the deadman's switch first, it goes off."

"And does what, exactly?" Leia asked.

"Makes a small thermonuclear fusion reaction," Dash answered.

"A small thermonuclear fusion reaction," she repeated.

"Yeah, just enough to vaporize a good-size chunk of whatever is next to it."

"I see. That includes us if it goes off in here, right?"

"Right. But we're betting your friend the leader of Black Sun won't want us to trigger it while he's around, not even to mention what it would do to his castle," Lando said, and smiled.

"You said you had more of them, right? I want to hang on to this one. It might come in handy," Leia said, and tucked the metal ball inside the bounty hunter's helmet hooked to her belt.

"Okay," Luke said with a shrug. "We bought it with your money anyway."

The blaster bolts outside the doorway stopped.

"I guess we better have a little talk with Xizor," Luke said.

Lando handed him another of the thermal detonators. Luke touched the controls. The device started beeping. Tiny lights winked on and off.

Luke took a deep breath.

Xizor followed the dozen or so guards who moved toward an open door across the hall from where he and Guri had ducked.

He heard a small noise, a repetitive beep. What was that?

Skywalker stepped out into the hall. The guards pointed their blasters, but the boy didn't have his lightsaber in hand. Instead, he held some kind of small device.

Xizor knew a bomb when he saw one.

"Don't shoot!" he yelled. "Lower your weapons!"

The guards looked at him as if he had gone mad, but they obeyed. The other intruders and Leia moved out into the hall behind Skywalker. The beeping was suddenly very loud in the silence. Tiny lights blinked on the device.

"You know what this is?" Skywalker said.

"I have a pretty good idea," Xizor said.

"It's rigged with a deadman's switch," Luke said. "If I let it go . . ."

There was no need to finish that sentence.

"What do you want?" Xizor asked.

"To leave. My friends and I."

"If you release the bomb, you'll die. So will your friends," Xizor said.

The boy shrugged. "The way it stands, we're dead anyway. We have nothing to lose. How about you? You ready to give all this up?" He waved at the building around them. "This is a Class A thermal detonator, you know what that means?"

"I think you're bluffing," Xizor said.

"Only one way to find out," Skywalker replied. "Your move."

Xizor thought about it. If the boy wasn't bluffing and somebody shot him, a Class A TD would take out several floors of this building in a heartbeat. With that many of the support girders erased, the eighty-odd stories above would collapse. The castle would be a total loss—as would anybody trapped inside it.

He could build another castle. But if the bomb went off this close, he wouldn't be around to do that. Was he willing to bet all he had worked for, his very life itself, that Skywalker was not suicidal?

No. He could not take the chance.

"All right. Leave. Nobody will stop you." Alive, he would be able to chase them down. Dead was dead.

Four of them edged past the guards, who nearly fell over themselves trying to get out of the way, as if a few meters would make any difference.

Skywalker stood facing him alone. Xizor watched the others walk away. Maybe Guri could move fast enough to grab the thing before it exploded.

Where was Guri?

He looked around. Suddenly the four stopped. The dark man reached into his pack and produced another shining ball.

Xizor smirked and said, "What's the point of that? You can't blow us up any more with two of those."

The man grinned. There was a garbage chute next to him, and he opened it. It led to the recycling bins in the sub-subbasement. He flipped a control on the device. It started beeping and flashing.

Xizor had an awful premonition. He yelled. "No!"

But Lando tossed the bomb into the chute.

"You have five minutes to leave the building," Lando said. "If I were you I'd get moving."

Xizor spun, faced his guards. "Get to the turbolifts, get to the basement and find that device! Get it out of here!"

But he was wasting his time. The guards panicked. They broke and ran, yelling frantically. They nearly knocked him over.

By the time he'd recovered, Skywalker and Leia and the others had gone, and the guards were hurrying to do the same.

Blast!

In five minutes Xizor's castle was going to be destroyed.

Xizor ran, too. He had a private express turbolift. If he hurried, he'd have plenty of time to get to his personal ship and get clear.

His emotions raged uncontrolled. A cold fire cooked his reason into deadly anger. He would get his ship, and he would follow them—to the end of the galaxy if he had to.

Then they were going to pay for this with their lives.

20

They took the lift and told it to hurry. Less than a minute later, they were on level fifty, with plenty of time to escape—if Threepio and Artoo had gotten there! If not, they weren't going to have long to regret it.

The doors opened and as they exited, twenty or thirty very excited people jammed in past them, stuffing the lift so full that there was no room left. Those people who couldn't make it cursed or screamed or cried, moved to the next turbolift door, and pounded on the call button.

"Must be quitting time," Dash observed.

"They have four whole minutes," Lando said, his voice dry. "Better hurry."

"That's cold," Luke said.

"They should have thought about that when they decided to go to work for Black Sun," Lando said. "It's a high-risk operation, being a crook."

"The landing pad ought to be that way," Dash said. "Come on."

Fifty meters down the hall, Luke heard something. He reached out with the Force, couldn't find anything. He waved the others on. "Go ahead, I'll be right there!" They did as he said.

He pulled his lightsaber out and flicked it on.

"Behold the Jedi Knight," a woman said. "The man of legend."

He turned. The woman called Guri stood there. A droid. Lando had described her in great detail on the way here.

"You have caused my master much misfortune," she said. "You should die for that."

Luke aimed the sword point at her. She didn't seem to be carrying any kind of weapon he could see, but Lando had told him how fast she was. And how strong.

"But you have that blade and I am unarmed," she said. She held her hands away from her sides, empty palms facing him.

He had maybe three minutes. The smart thing to do would be to cut her down and get moving. Or at least herd her out of the way using his sword and head for the rendezvous with—he hoped—the *Falcon*.

But why start doing the smart thing now?

He clicked the lightsaber off, rehooked it to his belt, and made sure it was securely fastened. "What do you want?"

"A test," she said. "My master pits himself against the deadliest opponents he can find. There are no men who are my equal in hand-to-hand combat. Except perhaps, if the stories are true, a Jedi Knight."

"This building is going to blow to pieces in three minutes," he said. "And you want to play games?"

"It won't take that long. Are you afraid to die, Skywalker?"

147

Yes, of course he was.

But then he realized that he really wasn't. The Force was with him. Whatever happened, happened. He spread his feet slightly and dropped into a fighting crouch. Guri smiled and slid into her own fighting stance.

She leaped at him, impossibly fast. On his own, he'd never have dodged, but he had the Force. He stepped to his right and kicked at her as she flew past. He hit her on the hip and knocked her sideways, but not off her feet.

"Luke!"

Leia's scream distracted him. He flicked his gaze toward the sound of her voice and saw her and the others turning to look at him. It was enough for Guri. She took a long, sliding step and punched. Luke backpedaled, but even so, her fist hit him in the belly hard.

She followed up with an elbow, but he dived away, rolled and turned, and came up with his hands lifted as she darted after him. He lost contact with the Force. He was on his own. She slapped him next to the ear and he went down, dazed.

If he didn't do something fast, she was going to kill him!

The Force. Let it work for you, Luke.

Luke heard Ben's voice calling as if from a great distance, echoing across time and space. He managed a breath as Guri raised her hand, formed now into a blade instead of a fist, a grin of triumph lighting her features.

Guri slowed, as if she were suddenly mired in time. He

saw her hand descend, saw it moving to smash him, but it was so incredibly slow, he could easily roll aside and stand before she ever reached him . . .

He did so. He felt as if he were moving at normal speed, though there was a crackling feeling to his motion, a sound like a strong wind whistling about his ears.

He came up, pivoted, thrust his open palm against the descending chop, and shoved it aside. He used his left leg, a sweep that caught Guri behind the right ankle. Her feet left the floor, still moving in slow motion, and she fell flat on her back . . .

Time speeded up.

Leia's yell still echoed down the corridor.

Guri hit the floor. He had never heard anybody fall that hard; it was a thump that shook him where he stood.

It stunned her.

Luke pulled his lightsaber and ignited it. This droid was deadly, too dangerous to remain in existence. He lifted the blade.

Lying on her back, stunned, she managed to smile. "You won fairly," she said. "Go ahead."

She would have finished you, he told himself. Time stalled again, stretched like plastic melting in a hot fire . . .

Luke lowered the blade and shut it off. "Come with us. We can have you reprogrammed."

She sat up. "No. If they can find a way around my brainblock, if somehow my memory is downloaded, it will be fatal for me—and my master. We have much to answer for. Better to kill me now."

"It's not your fault," he said. "You didn't program yourself."

"I am what I am, Jedi. I don't think there can be any salvation for me."

"Luke! Come on!"

He shook his head. "There's been enough killing," he said. "I'm not adding to it today." He nodded at her once, turned, and ran.

The five of them made it outside to the landing pad.

There was no sign of the *Millennium Falcon*.

Xizor's personal ship, the *Virago*, was on the top level. Since it was always kept fueled and ready to go, it needed no preparation. With the sounds of the emergency warning system braying over and over, he was somewhat surprised to see the ship guards still in place, although they were very nervous.

"The building is going to blow up," he said, as if talking about the weather. "Take one of the airspeeders and get away. You have two minutes to get clear."

The guards bowed and hurried away. Perhaps the failure of one was not the failure of all. These two guards would keep their jobs when this was done, maybe even get promoted. So rare to find loyalty these days.

He hurried onto the *Virago* and closed the hatch. He settled into the control seat, waved his hand over the computer sensors, and watched the screens light up. He would fly to his skyhook. He had his own navy stationed in and around the space station. He assumed those responsible for destroying his castle had a ship standing by to rescue them.

By the time that ship made it into orbit, his navy would be waiting.

"All systems go," the *Virago*'s computer said.

Good. He reached for the lift controls. More than a minute left.

He paused for a second, looking through the viewscreen at his castle. It was too bad about its destruction. He had spent many good years here, and he would miss it. But he would rebuild, a bigger, better, more majestic place. Until he could take over the Emperor's castle.

He touched the lift controls. The *Virago* rose smoothly from the pad and away into the bright sunshine.

He was a few hundred meters away, clear enough to be safe, when he saw a beat-up Corellian freighter coming at him. The ship seemed to be out of control. It corkscrewed on its horizontal axis, pitched and yawed.

Xizor cursed, hit his emergency boosters, and turned. The *Virago* jagged to port, then jumped as if kicked by a giant boot.

The incoming ship barely missed him.

What kind of idiot was in control of that vessel?

Dash saw it first. "Mother of Madness!" he yelled, pointing.

Luke looked up and saw the *Millennium Falcon,* coming in too fast and spinning like a demented top. As they watched, the wobbly ship straightened, but it was still coming in too fast.

"Duck!" Lando hollered.

The five of them dropped flat.

The ship pulled up no more than a meter from the pad's deck and veered to starboard. The wind of its passage tugged at them. Luke glanced up in the backwash just as the *Falcon*'s port edge hit a sensor dish and shattered it, spraying pieces every which way.

"Threepio, I'm gonna kill you!" Lando roared.

Luke came up with the others and watched the ship circle around. He pulled his comlink. "Threepio, cut your drives! Bring it in on the repulsors only! And hurry!"

"I'm trying, Master Luke. The controls are somewhat sensitive."

"Here she comes!" Dash said.

The *Falcon* drifted down toward them. They backed up. The ship hovered over the landing pad two meters up, then dropped like a stone. The landing struts groaned but held. The belly hatch's ramp yawned wide.

"Go, go, go!" Luke yelled.

Chewie grabbed Leia, picked her up, and ran. Dash and Lando were right behind, and Luke followed. Dash got to the cockpit first, Lando and Luke right behind him.

"Move!" Dash yelled at Threepio.

"I'm moving, I'm moving!"

There came a deep rumble from underneath them. The *Falcon* shook.

"Come on, Dash!" Lando yelled.

"Go, go!"

The *Millennium Falcon* spun away. As it did, Luke saw the building shake and the landing pad fall away, then drop straight down, like a tower of sand with the base kicked out. Smoke rose. A terrible screech like a giant nail being pulled from wet wood came with the smoke. Blasts of fire erupted skyward. Things exploded and hurled shrapnel at them.

Dash hit the thrusters, and the *Falcon* leaped upward.

Below, the castle of Xizor, Underlord of Black Sun, collapsed into a heap of flaming, smoking ruin. For once, even Lando didn't have a funny remark.

Leia joined the others in the crowded cockpit.

"Let's get out of here," Luke said. "Nothing fancy, just run as fast as we can."

"I hear you," Dash said.

21

Xizor was enraged. He had figured out that the small Corellian freighter that had nearly smashed into him as he leaped away from his castle was the same one his people had been searching for. The same one that had come to rescue Skywalker and Leia and their friends. He called ahead to his skyhook and ordered that it be destroyed.

"If it gets past, you and anybody else I consider responsible will be fertilizer before the next sunrise—are we perfectly clear on that?" he said.

"Clear, Prince Xizor."

"Good." He reached for the comm switch to shut off the transmission. "I've got you now, Skywalker."

"I beg your pardon, Highness?"

"Nothing. Never mind."

He flipped the switch and killed the transmission. He probably should not have mentioned Skywalker's name that way, but it didn't matter. The channel was scrambled. It did not matter. He was so close to finishing this now.

"My lord Vader, you asked to see anything regarding this name," the officer said.

Vader stared at the man. Took the printout from him and scanned it.

"Where did this originate?"

"An encoded transmission from the ship *Virago*, my lord, en route to the skyhook Falleen's Fist in high orbit. The ship is registered to—"

"I know who it is registered to," Vader said. "Make ready my shuttle."

He had warned Xizor to stay away from Luke. The criminal had chosen to ignore that order. That was a grievous error. As much as it was possible, Vader was delighted. They had played Xizor's game long enough. Now they would play his.

"Take over, would you, Luke?" Dash said.

"Sure." Luke, already in the copilot's seat, took the controls. "Where are you going?"

"Nowhere. I just need to whistle up my steed."

"What?"

Dash pulled a small, black, rectangular box from his belt. "Long-range shielded single-channel comlink. Time to have my droid Leebo put my ship into orbit. We can rendezvous, I can borrow one of your suits—this bucket still has vac-suits, doesn't it?—and get back to a real ship instead of this rickety crate."

"You really ought to consider signing on with the Alliance," Luke said. "You're a good man, and we could use you."

"Thanks, Luke, but I don't think so. I'm not much of a

joiner," Dash said. "Anyway, after this jaunt, I figure I've squared things with the Empire pretty well."

"Thanks for the ride," Dash said over the comm.

The *Outrider* hung just off the *Millennium Falcon*'s port bow in a matching orbit. Dash had jetted across the short gap, complaining all the while about how bad the borrowed suit smelled.

"Want to race to the jump spot?" Luke said. He now sat at the controls, taking a turn at piloting. Lando sat next to him; Leia stood behind them.

Dash laughed. "You want a parsec head start?"

A hard, green beam of light flashed between the two ships. Somebody was shooting at them.

"Uh-oh, looks like we got company."

Lando said, "We've got an unmarked corvette coming in at two-seventy! And four fighters at three-five-nine! Those aren't Imperial ships! Who are these guys?"

"Who cares?" Luke said. "We've got to move! Chewie, the guns!"

"You heard the man, furball," Leia said. "Shall we?"

Chewie snarled. He and Leia disappeared.

"Good luck, Dash!" Luke yelled.

"You too, Luke."

Luke pointed the *Falcon* into the deep and ran. The ship rocked as a beam found the shields and splashed from them.

They needed to get clear of this system, fast, and make the jump to hyperspace.

A beam hit them, slapped them crooked. The shields held.

Lando yelled into the comm. "I thought you two were supposed to be shooting back!"

Both Chewie and Leia yelled at him, but Luke was too busy flying to pay attention to what they said. He put the *Falcon* into a power climb and turned the move into a half twist at the top of the arc, heading back the way they'd come.

"Chewie wants to know how he's supposed to hit anything with you looping like that," Lando said.

"How can he miss? We're surrounded! He should hit something no matter where he shoots!"

A black shape zipped past them: the *Outrider*, cannons blazing.

Ahead of the *Falcon* a fighter exploded.

Lando said, "See how it's done, Chewie?"

Chewie yelled something back at Lando.

The attackers had them boxed. There didn't seem to be any way out. Too bad he couldn't get to his X-wing—though one more ship probably wouldn't be much help.

Things looked bad. Really bad . . .

One of the attacking fighters came straight at them, cannons winking hot plasma eyes. The attacker exploded. The *Falcon* blew through the cloud of debris. It pattered like hard rain against the shields.

"Good shot!" Luke yelled. "Who got it—was that you, Leia?"

"Not me," her voice came back. "I've got plenty to

worry about coming in from my side. Must have been Chewie."

Chewie said something.

Lando said, "Chewie says he didn't get it, either."

Luke blinked. Then who did?

Over the comm: "Hey, Luke! Okay if we join your party?"

"Wedge! What are you doing here?"

"Waiting for you. Dash's droid sent us a distress signal. Sorry it took so long to get here."

Another of the unmarked attackers blossomed into a fireball.

"Well, just don't let it happen again," Luke said. He grinned. Now that Rogue Squadron was here, the odds were a little better.

He swung the *Falcon* into a wide turn.

"There seems to be a slight problem, Highness," the commander said.

Xizor, watching the flashes of weapons and exploding ships from his deck, frowned. "So I noticed. Why are your ships blowing up, Commander?"

"A squadron of X-wing fighters has joined the fray. No more than a dozen of them. It will merely delay the inevitable."

"Are you certain, Commander?"

"We outnumber them twenty to one, Highness. Our frigates are standing by in case they get past the corvettes and fighters. They cannot escape."

"I hope you are right, Commander."

Vader stalked the bridge of the *Executor*.

"How long before we can get around the planet?" he asked.

"A few minutes, my lord," the nervous commander answered.

"As soon as we come within range, establish communications with the skyhook Falleen's Fist. I will speak with Prince Xizor."

"Of course, my lord."

"I think we got problems, buddy," Dash said. His voice was calm over the comm, but it was also resigned.

Luke nodded. "Wedge?"

"I'm afraid he's right, Luke. These guys are only so-so pilots, but there are a lot of 'em. I figure we're still outnumbered fifteen to one, and there are a couple of frigates that are just sitting there waiting. We don't have room to run, don't have room to maneuver. They're closing in, and they don't care if they kill civilian ships, either."

"Yeah," Luke said. He took a deep breath. "Well, I guess all we can do is take as many of them with us as we can. Unless anybody wants to surrender?"

Both Dash and Wedge laughed.

"That's what I thought. May the Force be with you."

Luke flew as he had never flown before. He weaved, rolled, stalled, dived, threw power turns that came close to blacking them all out. He was giving it his best, and he had the Force helping him, but they were losing.

It would only be a matter of time.

Suddenly Luke saw Imperial Navy TIE fighters screaming toward them. A dozen, at least.

"Uh-oh," said Lando.

"Yeah, I wondered what was keeping them." Luke looked at Lando. "Listen, thanks for everything, Lando. You've been a good friend."

"I don't want to hear that kind of talk. I still am a good friend."

Luke nodded and turned back to look at the TIE fighters. There was nowhere to go. It was like trying to fly through a hailstorm without being hit. He took a deep breath.

Luke saw the TIEs flash past and watched them take out two of the unmarked attackers.

"Huh?" Lando said.

"Luke," came Leia's voice over the comm, "I just saw—"

"I know, I know. What's going on?"

Xizor heard the panic in his commander's voice: "Highness, we're being attacked by the Imperial Navy!"

Next to him a communications tech waved frantically.

Xizor fixed the man with a baleful stare. "This had better be good. Your life hangs in the balance."

"It . . . It's Lord Vader. He wants to speak to you."

Vader! He should have known!

"Put him on."

Vader's image swirled into being in front of him. Xizor went on the offensive immediately: "Lord Vader! Why is the navy attacking my ships?"

There was a pause; then Vader said, "Because the ships, under your orders, are engaging in criminal activity."

"Nonsense! My ships are trying to stop a Rebel traitor who destroyed my castle!"

There came another pause. "You have two minutes to recall your vessels," Vader said. "And to offer yourself into my custody."

The coldness at Xizor's core blossomed uncontrolled into an angry heat. He tried to keep his voice calm. "I will not. I will take this up with the Emperor."

"The Emperor is not here. I speak for the Empire, Xizor."

"Prince Xizor."

"You may keep the title—for another two minutes."

Xizor forced a confident smile. "What are you going to do, Vader? Destroy my skyhook? You wouldn't dare. The Emperor—"

"I warned you to stay away from Skywalker. Recall your ships and surrender into my custody or pay the consequences."

The commander of Xizor's navy put in a frantic call to his master. Vader listened to the decoded communication over the speaker system.

"My prince, we are being destroyed by the attackers! We are outnumbered and being slaughtered! I need permission to offer our surrender! Highness?"

Vader watched the chronometer, enjoyed the time melting away. Not much left for the Dark Prince now.

Seven seconds . . . six seconds . . . five . . .

The terrified commander kept babbling: "Prince Xizor, please respond! We must surrender or we will be blown to pieces! Please!"

Four seconds left . . . three seconds . . .

"Highness, I—" the commander's transmission ended abruptly. One of the Imperial fighters must have gotten him.

Two . . . one—

"Commander, destroy the skyhook," Vader ordered.

One did not stay in command of Darth Vader's ship by questioning orders. "Yes, my lord."

Darth Vader took a deep breath, painful as it was to do so, and let it out slowly. He smiled, unseen.

Goodbye, Xizor. And good riddance.

As it happened, the *Millennium Falcon* was facing it when the skyhook exploded.

Luke saw the giant Star Destroyer's powerful beam strobe, saw it pierce the skyhook. The planetoid shattered, blew apart, and went nova. It became a small star that burned brightly for an instant before it faded, leaving millions of glowing pieces behind.

It was a spectacular sight for all its violence. It reminded Luke of the explosion that destroyed the Death Star.

"Oh, man," Lando said softly. "They must have made somebody real mad."

Luke shook his head and didn't speak.

Dash said, "Heads up, boys. Follow me."

Luke blinked. "Huh?"

"Somebody just opened us an escape hatch."

"Are you crazy? We can't fly through that wreckage!"

"What's the matter, kid? Don't think you can do it?"

"If you can, my droid could. Go."

Luke understood what Dash meant. It would be tricky, dangerous, but the space around the destroyed skyhook was relatively clear. If they could avoid being smashed by the debris, this was their best chance.

They headed for the debris, and it looked as if it was going to be just fine. The good guys had triumphed!

"Look out, Dash!" Lando yelled.

Luke could hardly spare a glance, but he did—just in time to see a block of shattered skyhook smash into the *Outrider*.

"Dash!" Luke yelled.

There was a flare of light too bright to look at. Luke turned away, saw Lando throw one arm up to block the glare.

When the light faded, the *Outrider* had vanished.

"Oh, man," Lando said. "He—he's . . . gone."

Just like that.

The sweet taste of triumph went bitter in Luke's mouth.

There wasn't time to worry about it now. "Brace yourselves! This is going to be rough!"

The debris flashed around them, impacts waiting at every turn. He was sorry about Dash—the man had turned out to be okay after all—but he didn't want to end up a pile of flaming rubble. He let the Force take him and flew.

The secret Alliance base was light years away from Imperial Center. They had barely made it.

Luke stood with Leia, Lando, and Chewie, with Threepio and Artoo behind them. The building was, like so many of the Alliance structures, a big, cheap prefab unit. It did boast a large viewscreen facing out from the surface of the asteroid into the blackness of space. Luke stared through the thick transparisteel into the depths of the galaxy.

"So, if Xizor was on that skyhook like our intelligence reports say, I would guess that would put a stop to Black Sun bounty hunters looking to kill you," Lando said.

"There's still Vader," Leia said.

Luke looked at her and shook his head. "I don't think Vader wants me dead. Not yet, anyway. I'll deal with him when the time comes."

They looked up to see Wedge approaching. "Got a message for you, Luke," Wedge said. "From the Bothans. It was for Dash, but, well . . ." He trailed off. "Anyway, that missile Dash supposedly missed during that fracas off Kothlis? Turns out he didn't miss."

"What?" Luke blinked at Wedge.

"It was one of the Empire's new diamond-boron-armored jobs. Nothing he had to throw at it could have stopped it. The Bothans wanted him to know."

Luke was stunned. *Oh, man.* Dash hadn't screwed up, but now he would never know. How awful, to get taken out before you could learn that you hadn't been responsible for the loss of your comrades.

"What are you going to do now?" Wedge said.

"We're going to get Han," Luke said. "If he isn't on Tatooine yet, he soon will be."

"Going to dance into the Hutt's guarded palace and get him? Just like that?" Wedge said.

"I have a plan," Luke said.

He turned and looked at the stars. Maybe he wasn't a Master yet, but he had learned a lot.

He was a Jedi Knight, and that was enough for now.

EPILOGUE

In the Emperor's most private sanctum, Darth Vader knelt before his master. He believed he had reason to be worried.

"You defied my orders, Lord Vader," the Emperor said menacingly.

"Yes, my master. But I hope I have not failed you."

"Get up."

Vader stood.

The Emperor favored Vader with a dark smile. "I am not unaware that Xizor served his own ends and that you were shrewd to have uncovered his plot. I knew about it, of course."

Vader did not speak.

The Emperor smiled again. "Are we certain he is dead?"

"I do not see how he could have survived. I watched his skyhook blown to bits."

"Just as well. Black Sun is useful, but it is also like a chirru. Cut off its head and another will appear to replace it." He cackled, amused at his own metaphor.

"Perhaps the next leader will be equally dangerous," Vader said.

"No leader of Black Sun could ever be a match for the power of the dark side."

"But what of the plot to ensnare the Rebel leaders?"

"The new Death Star will draw them in, and this time you and I will be there to finish this Rebellion."

Vader wanted to shake his head. As always, the Emperor was one step ahead of him.

"Young Skywalker will be there, too. I have foreseen it."

Vader sighed.

"It is all proceeding exactly as I have foreseen it, Lord Vader."

Vader felt a chill touch him. Truly there was no one in the galaxy who had control of the dark side as did the Emperor. It was a weakness in Vader that he could feel that fear. Some part of Anakin Skywalker still existed in him, despite all he had done. He would have to eliminate it or it would eventually be his undoing.

In Ben's house on Tatooine, Luke took a deep breath and reached for calmness. They didn't expect Jabba would be interested in the proposal, given what they had learned about how nasty he was. If the Hutt were willing to negotiate, it would save a lot of trouble, but none of them really expected it. Jabba was, according to all they'd learned, extremely mean-spirited, and he didn't need the money. Too bad.

Oh, well. They'd just have to do things the hard way. What else was new?

"Okay, Artoo, start recording."

Artoo bleeped.

"Greetings, exalted one. Allow me to introduce myself. I am Luke Skywalker, Jedi Knight and friend to Captain Solo. I know that you are powerful, mighty Jabba, and that your anger with Solo must be equally powerful. I seek an audience with Your Greatness to bargain for Solo's life."

If what they'd heard was true, Jabba would probably start laughing about now. Luke paused for a moment, caught his breath, and went on:

"With your wisdom, I'm sure that we can work out an arrangement which will be mutually beneficial and enable us to avoid any unpleasant confrontation."

Small chance of that. But he pressed on:

"As a token of my goodwill, I present to you a gift—these two droids."

Luke fought the grin that threatened him: No doubt whatsoever that Threepio would be stunned to hear this when the recording was played. Luke had considered telling him but thought it would be better if he didn't know. He got rattled so easily. Besides, Threepio's surprise would help convince Jabba.

"Both are hardworking and will serve you well," Luke finished.

He glanced at Artoo and raised an eyebrow, and the little droid shut his recorder off.

Leia, standing behind Artoo, shook her head. "You think that will do it?"

Luke shrugged. "I hope so. Only one way to find out."

She moved closer and touched his arm.

Luke said, "Hey, after all we just went through, rescuing one beat-up old pirate ought to be easy, right?"

She smiled. "Right."

Hang on, Han.

We're coming for you.